THE ROBE OF SKULLS

The First Tale from
THE FIVE KINGDOMS

THE ROBE OF SKULLS

VIVIAN FRENCH

ILLUSTRATED BY ROSS COLLINS

SCHOLASTIC INC.
New York Toronto London Auckland
Sydney Mexico City New Delhi Hong Kong

ISBN-13: 978-0-545-21148-2
ISBN-10: 0-545-21148-4

Text copyright © 2007 by Vivian French.
Illustrations copyright © 2007 by Ross Collins. All rights reserved.
Published by Scholastic Inc., 557 Broadway, New York, NY 10012, by arrangement with Candlewick Press. SCHOLASTIC and associated logos are trademarks and/or registered trademarks of Scholastic Inc.

12 11 10 9 8 7 6 5 4 3 2 1   9 10 11 12 13 14/0

Printed in the U.S.A.   40

First Scholastic printing, September 2009

This book was typeset in Baskerville.

Dearest Sue, this book's for you.

Chapter One

"Skulls," said Lady Lamorna. "Definitely skulls. Rows and rows of dear little skulls, sewn all along the hem." She sighed with pleasure as she imagined the clitter-clatter of bone on her cold stone floors. "After all, it really is time I had a new gown. Black velvet, of course, and long . . . very long. Perhaps embroidered? Hmm . . . yes. A motif of spiders, or maybe twists of poison ivy." Her huge silver eyes gleamed. "In fact, why not interweave the ivy with spiders' webs? That would be truly beautiful. And petticoats. Layers and layers of blood-red petticoats . . . oh, yes, yes, YES! It will be a robe beyond all compare, and I shall order it this very minute!"

Lady Lamorna snapped her long bony fingers, and within seconds a sharp-toothed bat came flipping in through the open window.

"Yup?"

"I have an order for the Ancient Crones," Lady Lamorna said. "I require a new robe, edged with skulls—"

"Got it." The bat made a swift circle over the Lady's head. "Skulls, velvet, webs, ivy, petticoats. No prob. Delivery date?"

Lady Lamorna looked put out. "Bat! Listen to me! I would like a new robe, made of deep-black velvet—"

"Told ya. I got it." The bat circled again. "Heard you a mile away. I'm a bat, right? Bat ears 'n' all that stuff. Now—delivery?"

Lady Lamorna gave up. "As soon as possible," she said stiffly.

"Roger Wilco. I'll be back soon with info on price and delivery. Have the readies ready. Coins of all denominations readily accepted. *Ciao!*" And the bat whizzed away into the purple twilight.

For a second, Lady Lamorna considered frizzling the bat to a burnt ember as it flew, but then she remembered her delicious dress. With a smile of happy anticipation, she swept toward her treasure chest, flung open the lid . . . and SCREAMED!

* * *

They still talk about that scream in the high mountain village of Fracture. Dogs howled and bit their owners. Cats' whiskers curled into corkscrews and fell off. Children clutched their ears and shrieked in agony. Only the old and extremely deaf were spared . . . the old, the extremely deaf, and Gracie Gillypot. Gracie had been shut in her stepfather's cold, dark, and spidery cellar for being cheerful, and the cellar had very thick walls. Even in the cellar she heard a faint cry and wondered what it could be—but her ears did nothing worse than tingle. Her stepsister, Foyce, caught the full blast, and when Gracie was finally allowed out of the cellar, Foyce slapped her several times because her head felt as if it were full of stinging wasps, and she didn't like it.

Gubble, crouched only a few yards away from Lady Lamorna as she hit the highest and most piercing note of her scream, sighed heavily. He'd been the Lady's servant for more than 170 years, and he had heard her scream before. He knew what the scream meant. It meant trouble.

"*Poor* Gubble," he said to himself. "Trouble coming. Trouble for Gubble." He shook his head and began to suck his large grubby thumb.

Five minutes later, he realized what he had said. A huge self-congratulatory smile spread across his flat green face. "Trouble for Gubble!" he said, and the smile grew even wider. "*Clever* Gubble! Gubble's a POTE!" And he chuckled happily.

It was lucky for Gubble that Lady Lamorna didn't hear him. A hundred and seventy years of faithful service would have meant nothing if she'd seen him smiling, let alone chuckling. Fortunately, she was pacing the battlements of her crumbling castle, muttering as she stared out across the rooftops of the village.

"Money! Money! Money! Gold! Silver! Pennies, even! How can it *be* that my treasure box is empty? And how can I pay the crones for my beautiful, magical dress?" The Lady tugged at a lock of her long white hair. "Hmm. I could send fool's gold, but fool's gold lasts for one month only . . . and the Ancient Crones will strike me down with thunderbolts if they find I have paid with nothing but pebbles . . ."

Lady Lamorna stamped her foot in frustration and fury and swung back inside. "Gubble!" she called. *"Gubble!"*

Gubble half hopped, half hobbled from the dark cupboard that was his usual resting place.

"What skills do I have, Gubble?" Lady Lamorna

demanded. "What skills that will earn me a fortune in good strong gold?"

Gubble shook his head.

"*Think*, Gubble!"

Gubble opened and shut his toothless mouth. He could see by the glint in Lady Lamorna's silver eyes that Gubble's Trouble was extraordinarily near now, all ready to jump. Gubble gulped. He wasn't entirely certain that he actually knew what *skills* were . . . but at the last second some kind of association of sounds dropped another word into his head—a word he knew his mistress liked. "Spells, Your Evilness," he said. "Spells." A happy memory came to him. "That frog thing you do. Prince. *Zap!* Frog." Gubble's piggy little eyes shone. "That be *magnifying*!"

"Fool! You mean *magnificent*!" snapped Lady Lamorna, but she didn't sound nearly as menacing as she usually did when Gubble got things wrong. He heaved a sigh of relief as she strode across the room and seized a black marble urn from her mantelpiece. Peering inside, she nodded. "If we are economical, Gubble, there is sufficient spell powder for at least a dozen transformations."

Gubble looked vacant.

Lady Lamorna tapped sharply on the heavy oak

coffin lid she used as a table. Underneath, in the coffin, the bones of her great-grandmother, the first Lady Lamorna, rattled loudly, and there was a hollow laugh.

"Good," said the living Lady. "Great-Grandmother approves. Now, Gubble—we've established that my ability to turn princes into frogs is a valuable asset. So—how do we progress with this idea?"

Gubble stared blankly at his mistress. He'd understood *princes* and *frogs,* and his ears always pricked up when the word *valuable* came into a conversation, but he had no idea what the Lady wanted now. For the second time in one day, he cast wildly about in the small foggy compartment where his brain got on with its own private life. Mostly it was busy with *murder,* or *blood,* or *violent death,* but Gubble managed to track down something that seemed to suit the occasion. "Toast!" he said. Then, seeing Lady Lamorna's face darken, he hastily added, "*And* marmalade."

Lady Lamorna slapped Gubble. His head spun off his shoulders and thunked onto the floor.

"Urk!" grunted the head. And then, completely amazing Lady Lamorna and dazzling Gubble himself, the head made a suggestion. "Blackmail." His mistress positively gasped. "Gubble!" she said. "I could *kiss* you!"

The head rolled away as fast as it could into a dusty corner. "Nah!" it whimpered. "Not *kisses!*" And it hid its nose in a convenient cobweb.

Lady Lamorna wasn't listening. She had seized a piece of paper and was wildly scribbling. She took no notice at all as Gubble's head and body silently edged toward each other and were reunited.

Chapter Two

Gracie Gillypot stood and stirred the saucepan of boiling water on the old iron stove. Maybe, she said to herself, maybe if she imagined as hard as she possibly could, it might taste of roast beef. Or chicken. Or tomatoes. Or even cabbage. Anything would be better than water soup. They'd had water soup every night for the last three days, and it wasn't improving her stepfather's temper. Mange Undershaft had started to shut her in the cellar every time he saw her smiling, and he'd threatened that if he ever heard her laughing, he'd keep her down there for a week. Gracie sighed. She didn't mind too much if she was put in the cellar during the day; once her eyes got used to the dim light from the grating, she could see her way around. But it was different in the evening. It was horribly dark and creepy, and it was all she could do not to burst into tears and wail miserably. It was only the thought of how delighted Mange would be if he thought he'd made her cry that stopped her, but it was getting harder and harder to stay brave. She'd had to bury her face in her hankie to stifle her sniffing just the night before . . . but then a bat had come swooping in for a chat, and that had cheered her up.

"Hi, kiddo!" the bat had said. "Come here often?"

"Much *too* often," Gracie said with feeling.

The bat flew swiftly around the cellar and settled on the handle of a broken spade. "Seems OK to me," he said cheerfully.

"It's all right for you," Gracie said. "*You* can see in the dark. I can't. And I'm sure the spiders are sniggering at me."

"That's really something." The bat sounded impressed. "Never heard them myself. Always thought they had a sense-of-humor bypass. What are you doing down here, anyway?"

"My stepdad doesn't like me laughing," Gracie explained. "Or smiling. I made water soup for supper, and I was trying to be cheerful about it, and he got horribly angry and threw me and the soup down here together."

"Correct me if I'm wrong," said the bat, "but would the main ingredient of water soup be water?"

Gracie nodded. "I do use hot water *and* cold water. It doesn't make much difference in the taste, though."

There was a moment's silence. Gracie wondered if the bat had flittered away, but then he said, "Are you hungry, kiddo?"

Gracie was so hungry she didn't know what to say. She'd been hungry for days and weeks and months and years. In fact, she couldn't remember a single moment in the whole of her life when she hadn't been hungry. She said, "Yes."

"Thought so. I'll see what I can do. Won't be same-day delivery, mind you."

"*Any* day delivery would be just wonderful," Gracie said.

"Check. Be seeing you soon, then. *Ciao!*" There was the faintest sound, and the bat was gone.

Gracie pulled at her pigtails thoughtfully. How could a very small bat deliver anything that would go even the smallest way to making her feel as if she'd eaten?

"Oi! Kiddo!" The bat was outside the grating. "If an alternative position were offered, would you be up for it?"

"What?" Gracie stared into the darkness.

"Something different. Change of employment. New line. Different boss."

Gracie was about to say that she wasn't employed by anyone, but then a whole new thought clanged into her head. The bat was right. She did have a boss. Mange might be her stepfather, but he was all "step" and no "father." All he ever did was order her around. And Foyce . . . Gracie bit her lip. Her stepsister, Foyce, was as mean as both of Cinderella's sisters rolled into one, but she wasn't ugly. She was dazzlingly beautiful, with a heart as hard as a frying pan.

"I'd certainly be interested," she told the bat. "In fact, very interested."

"Great. No prob there, then. See ya, kiddo!" And this time the bat was really gone.

Gracie strained her ears to see if she could hear him, but the silence was overwhelming. She sat down on a heap of kindling to wait for Mange to remember her and let her out. As she waited, she thought about the bat and wondered what he had in mind.

Chapter Three

Gracie was still wondering as she stirred her soup the following day. There hadn't been any sign of the bat, and she was beginning to believe she'd imagined the whole thing. After all, how likely was it that a talking bat would come flitting into Mange Undershaft's cellar? Any bat that was intelligent enough to talk would surely keep clear. Everything else did. Even second-class zombies never knocked on the door to offer badly made packages of hauntings and screechings. Word had gotten around, and Mange's door was the most unknocked-on in Fracture. All the same, Gracie had packed her few belongings into an old shawl and hidden them under the sink. Just in case.

"Pssssst! Kiddo!"

Gracie jumped.

The bat was hovering outside the open back door. In one claw it was holding a small cloth bag. "Here!" he said. "Dump this in your soup! And get your gear ready. We've got liftoff tonight!"

Gracie took the little bag with trembling fingers. "Thank you," she said. "Thank you *very* much!"

"Just remember—don't crack a smile," the bat instructed. "I can't get you out of the cellar. Keep frowning! *Ciao!*" And it vanished.

As Gracie untied the little bag, a strange smell began to fill the room. It was the smell of a rich meaty stew . . . previously quite unknown in that cold bare kitchen. Gracie tipped the gray powder into the boiling water. At once the smell grew ten times stronger, and the water bubbled and thickened. As she went on stirring, the soup turned a glorious deep brown, and chunks of beef and onions and mushrooms and buttery potatoes filled the saucepan to the very top.

"Wow!" Gracie breathed softly. "Wow! Thank you, bat!"

Crash!

The door slammed shut as Mange arrived in a rush, his thin bony nose twitching. "Food!" he growled. "And about time, too! Dish it out, dung beetle!"

Gracie began to ladle the stew into three bowls, but Mange snatched the spoon from her hand.

"And what have *you* done to deserve a supper?" He picked up the third bowl and dropped it on the stone floor.

As it smashed into a thousand pieces, Foyce followed her father into the kitchen. She paused in the doorway and sniffed the air. "Is that *food*?" she asked, and as always, Gracie found herself wondering how such a clear silvery voice could sound so evil. "And where *exactly* did the little slug find food like this?"

Gracie didn't answer, and neither did Mange. He was far too busy slurping stew into his mouth. Foyce came closer to the saucepan and pinched Gracie's arm. "Tell me," she said. "Tell me where it came from, or I'll tell Pa to put you in the cellar till your bones rot."

Gracie was saved from answering by Mange leaping up to refill his bowl. "Start eating, princess," he spluttered through a mouthful. "You can pinch her afterward. It's good stuff!"

Foyce let Gracie go but gave her a calculating stare

as she sat down across from her father. "She's been up to something, Pa," she said. "Look at her sneaky face! And if you ask me, it's magic, and if she's gotten hold of any magic, she should hand it over to *us*!"

"Umph," said Mange. "More stew!" And he filled his bowl for the third time.

"See?" Foyce told him. "That pan's filling up as soon as you empty it. It's like I told you. She's found some magic. Put her in the cellar, Pa."

"Got to eat first," Mange said without moving.

"Then I'll do it," Foyce said. "Something's odd around here. I know it is!" And she began to get up from the table.

Gracie backed away, her heart pounding. Should she make a dash for it now? Should she run out of the door and hope the bat would find her? She knew she didn't have much chance of getting away. Foyce had long legs and could run like the wind.

Gracie decided to try to distract her stepsister instead. *"Please!"* she begged in her whiniest voice. "Please, dear Foyce—*please* let me have some stew! Just a very little bit—*please*!" Gracie's begging was genuine. Her stomach was tying itself in knots, and the smell of the stew was driving her mad with hunger.

"Not likely, slug." Foyce gave a triumphant glare and began to eat. She had hardly finished her second mouthful when Mange slumped onto the table, snoring loudly.

"Pa?" Foyce shook his arm. "*Pa!* Wake up!"

Mange didn't move.

Foyce tried to leap to her feet but couldn't. She felt heavy . . . very heavy indeed . . . and she rubbed her eyes furiously to stop them from closing. "You little toad!" she screeched at Gracie. "You've poisoned us! Just you wait until I catch you. . . . I'll make your life so miserable you'll wish you were—" Her head flopped, and she began to snore almost as loudly as her father.

Gracie looked wistfully at the magic stew. She was *so* hungry, but she certainly didn't want to risk falling into an enchanted sleep and waking up beside a vengeful Foyce. Or Mange. She moved across to the back door and opened it to see if the fresh evening air would blow away the mouthwatering aroma of meat and onions . . . and the bat flipped in with a cheery "Hi, babe! Enjoy your dinner?"

Gracie shook her head. "I haven't eaten any yet. Won't it make me go to sleep?"

"You?" The bat's eyes widened as he settled on the back of a chair. "Never! Didn't you read the label?"

"Erm . . . no. Sorry." Gracie fished in the trash for the twist of cloth and peered at it. Something was written in the most minute handwriting, and she had to screw up her eyes to read it.

TRUEHEART STEW
Add to boiling water and stir.
WARNING:
A noble beef and vegetable stew
for the true of heart.
For others, a powerful sleeping potion.

"WOW," Gracie said, and hurried to the stove. "That's so clever!" She seized a spoon and looked at the bat. "Would you like some?"

"Nah. Thanks all the same." The bat shifted uneasily. "Never been too certain of the state of the old heart. Dodgy deals are my business, see."

Gracie dug a spoon into the saucepan and began to eat hungrily. "What kind of deals?" she asked.

The bat shook his head. "You don't want to know. Nothing evil, mind you. I don't do evil. Just dodgy. Now, get that inside you, and we'll be off."

"That was totally delicious!" Gracie said as she polished off her last spoonful of stew. Tidy to the last, she put the spoon and saucepan in the sink before pulling out the bundle she'd hidden underneath. "I'm ready now. Where are we going?"

The bat glanced over his shoulder, as if expecting to be overheard. "The Ancient Crones," he whispered.

"Wow!" Gracie said, and shivered. "I thought they were supposed to be scary. . . ."

"They are," said the bat. "Now, let's go!" He flittered out the back door and Gracie hurried after him.

Foyce heaved her head off the table. "Shneaky little rat shrunning away, eh?" she said thickly. "Well, well, well. We'll shee about that!" And she pulled her warm fur-lined cloak from the hook on the door and staggered after Gracie.

Chapter Four

Lady Lamorna looked at her map and frowned. "The Kingdom of Gorebreath. The Kingdom of Dreghorn. The Kingdom of Cockenzie Rood. The Kingdom of Wadingburn. The Kingdom of Niven's Knowe. Is that five, Gubble? Or six?"

Gubble, who hadn't been listening, nodded hard. "Six, Your Evilness. Unless it be five, that is. It'll be five unless it be six."

Lady Lamorna threw her inkpot at his head. "Fool! Pay attention! Now, if there are five kingdoms, there will, I hope, be five princes. Or princesses. All of them doted on by their fond and loving mamas and papas . . . *yeuch*. Now, Gubble, my plan is to infiltrate the palaces and, quite unsuspected by the royal parents, place an amphibian enchantment on each merry little heir to the throne. I will then send a letter"—

Lady Lamorna waved a piece of paper scrawled over and over with her jagged handwriting—"a letter, which I have already composed, offering my services as an enchantress of the *very* highest order. In return for *large* sums of money, to be paid only in solid gold pieces, I will restore their beloved offspring to their original state. Of course, they will then be so very, *very* grateful that I will be rewarded again, even more handsomely, thus providing more than adequate sums to pay for my beautiful dress. Is that not a truly amazing and extraordinary scheme, Gubble?"

Gubble, ink dripping off the end of his nose, opened and shut his mouth a few times in the hope that something clever might come out. Nothing did. "Ah," he said at last. "Gold pieces is good, Your Evilness. Very good. Very, *very* good."

"And my plan, Gubble!" Lady Lamorna began to tap her foot in an ominous fashion. "My plan—isn't *that* good?"

Gubble did his best to think what plan she was talking about. As he could only think of one, he settled for that. "Yeah. Yeah, Your Evilness. The frog plan is good. I likes the frog plan." The foot stopped tapping and Gubble relaxed. "Fantasticult, that plan is. Prince. *Zap!* Frog." A wide grin spread over his face.

"Gubble," said Lady Lamorna, "I do believe losing your head has made you more intelligent. Well done. Now, we must set off tomorrow morning early." She glanced at her map. "I suggest we start with the Kingdom of Dreghorn. It's by far the nearest. You go and prepare everything we need for our journey, and I will make my own preparations for my disguise." She gathered up the map and handed it to Gubble with a flourish. "Here, take care of this. Do *not* lose it! It is at least a hundred years since I last left this castle, and my memory may fail me. So many of these foolish little kingdoms have sprung up of late. Now, after Dreghorn we will go to Wadingburn, and so on and so on until our mission is complete. Oh—and Gubble—be sure to bring a donkey. Or even two. The gold will be heavy!" And Lady Lamorna swept away, rubbing her bony hands together in anticipation of the enormous wealth to come.

Gubble was left standing in a puddle of black ink and blacker confusion. He scratched his ear, but it didn't help. He began to scratch the other ear, but the map got in his way. "Umph," he said crossly. He screwed up the sheet of parchment and stuffed it into his mouth, then scratched the other ear thoroughly. "Donkeys," he said. "Donkeys. Must pack donkeys."

And with a gloomy feeling that there was a great deal more to it than donkeys, he stomped off to help himself to two sturdy animals from the nearest farm. Behind him, Great-Grandmother Lamorna arranged her bones more comfortably in her coffin and sighed.

Chapter Five

Prince Marcus, second in line to the throne of Gorebreath, was busy. He was arranging a booby trap for his twin brother, Prince Arioso, but even as he balanced the bucket of soapy water on top of the door, he knew it would be a disappointment. His twin— older by exactly ten minutes and thus first in line to the throne—was so boringly good, he would probably thank Marcus for providing him with a delightful shower. "What a totally charming surprise!" he would say, and then wander away to do extra homework.

Marcus shook his head. It was seriously weird, he thought. They had the same mom. The same dad. They were twins. They looked so alike that only their parents could tell them apart, and even they got it wrong sometimes . . . and yet he and Arioso were so different. Arry did everything he was told and never complained. He studied books and books about royalty and kingdoms without a murmur of protest. He went out with their parents in the royal coach and bowed and waved to the adoring crowds, and said he'd enjoyed every minute. He let whiskery old women kiss him without complaining. He even picked up soggy babies and let them dribble down his neck, and then said, "Goo goo goo—who's a pretty baby?"

Marcus shuddered. The worst of it was, they could have had such a good time. That was what twins were meant for. Every now and again Marcus would dress up in Arioso's silks and satins and ride down to the town on his snow-white horse and stir things up a bit, but it wasn't much fun doing it on your own. In fact, it wasn't any fun at all. There was always some depressingly wise old woman behind a market stall who'd say, "Aha! You be Prince Marcus, ain't ee? Us never sees Good Prince Arry snitching apples or letting the piggies out of their pens. Still, boys will be boys. You enjoy yourself, my duckling, and I'll be a-sending of the bill to the Palace as usual."

Marcus finished balancing the bucket and wandered away to the palace window. Staring out at the carefully tended gardens and the rows of statues of exceptionally noble knights, he thought for the millionth time that being a prince was about the most boring thing anyone could ever be. Endless receptions, banquets, balls, and garden parties were bad enough, but then there were all the lessons he and Arry were expected to sit through. Marcus sighed. He was meant to be studying *The Rules of Royal Etiquette When Entertaining Persons of Dubious Respectability,* but Professor Scallio had wandered out of the library and Marcus had made his escape. Arry, no doubt, was still sitting in the middle of a pile of books making copious notes in his homework notebook. It would have been fractionally more interesting, Marcus thought gloomily, if there were even the faintest chance of a Person of Dubious Respectability coming within a thousand miles of the palace . . . but the last recorded visit of any seriousness (a charity collector who had made off with the Royal Treasure Chest and King Frank's train set) had been years and years ago. As it was, the only people who ever came to the castle were the kings and queens and princes and princesses from Dreghorn or Cockenzie Rood or the other kingdoms scattered across the Northern Plains. Marcus was depressingly certain that there wasn't a Dubious Person within a thousand miles. Annoying—yes. Bigheaded—yes. Pompous? Marcus groaned. Oh, *yes*! But mostly boring, boring, *boring*. If he were Arry, he'd declare war on all of them just as soon as he reached twenty-one—

Crash!

The bucket fell off the door, and water splashed everywhere in the most satisfactory fashion. Marcus jumped up hopefully and saw a dripping Professor Scallio standing in the doorway.

"Oops," Marcus said. "Sorry, Professor—that was meant for Arry."

"Is that so," the professor said sourly. "Well, Prince Marcus, I have a task meant for *you*. You can write out the famous Gorebreath saying, *'A wise man balances a bucket where only the thirsty walk,'* five hundred times. I shall expect the lines to be on my desk by six o'clock this evening. If you fail in this task, I shall tell your father, the king, that you are *not* to ride out with your brother tomorrow morning. Ah!" Professor Scallio slapped his forehead. "Speaking of your father reminds me. I came to tell you that you are wanted in the throne room." And the tutor turned and trudged away.

"Oh, *rats!*" Marcus said loudly, and kicked savagely at the metal bucket to release his feelings. He hated upsetting Professor Scallio. The fat little tutor had a sharp tongue when he was angry, but he was one of the few people who treated Marcus in exactly the same way he treated Arioso. In fact, Marcus had even wondered once or twice if the professor didn't actually prefer him to Arry. Sometimes, when Arry gave his sweet smile for the tenth time in a morning and said, "I'm sure you must be right, Professor—you know *so* much more than I do," the tutor would bite his lip and frown. But when Marcus challenged him and argued a point to the death and beyond, Professor Scallio's eyes would shine and he'd wave his arms so enthusiastically that he seemed to be about to take off. And his punishments were often almost a pleasure. He regularly sent Marcus to spend his free time dusting the least-used section of the library—a dark and gloomy alcove where moths fluttered wildly at the sound of a human step and bats flew from the top shelf with squeaks of protest. Marcus had found several ancient tomes describing dragon fights and battles with werewolves, and a battered collection of recipes for poisoning sea serpents. He'd even found an ancient map of the mountains and forests that lay beyond his father's kingdom. Geography was not a subject that Arry and Marcus were encouraged to study. The king had forbidden the professor to teach them about anything other than local kingdoms. Arry, of course, accepted this as gracefully as he always did any rule or regulation, but Marcus had fought hard . . . with no success. Professor Scallio refused to answer a single one of his questions about what happened over the borders of Gorebreath. The map was Marcus's most exciting find and he was happy to have any opportunity to look at it again, so dusting was not something he complained about. Lines, however, were a very real and nasty punishment.

Marcus slammed the parlor door shut behind him and stomped off to see why he was wanted in the throne room. Five hundred lines! He'd *never* get them done by six—not if he was going to do as he had promised and help Ger, the stable boy, groom the horses.

"Oh, *rats!*" he said to himself. "That means no riding tomorrow . . . although I don't remember Arry saying anything about me coming with him." He shook his head. "Thought he was going to some la-di-da do in Dreghorn. . . ."

Marcus jumped the last seven steps and thumped his way into the throne room, scowling and angry. He bowed sketchily to his parents and saw Arry standing beside them, smiling his widest smile.

"Aha!" King Frank said cheerfully. "The missing prince! We've got some exciting news for you, Marcus old boy!"

"If you say so, Father." Marcus didn't even try to sound interested. He knew from much experience that what his father considered exciting was rarely anything other than just plain boring.

"There's a change of plans for tomorrow. Such fun!" King Frank's eyes were shining. "You know Arioso was invited to Princess Fedora's birthday party? Well, we've just had a message to say that we're *all* expected!" He waved a piece of parchment covered in crests and seals under Marcus's nose. "Young Fedora's gone and gotten herself engaged to Prince Tertius of Niven's Knowe, so the party's turned into a celebration for everybody! Wild rejoicing at noon, ringing of church bells at three, more rejoicing at four, and free beer for the peasants at six o'clock sharp. Messenger says there'll be dancing till dawn—good stuff, eh?"

"Um." Marcus was not enthused by the program of celebratory events. "I don't suppose there'll be jousting, will there? Or trials of strength?"

"Of course not," his mother said sharply. "It's the celebration of an engagement, Marcus. That means love and happiness, not biffing and bopping. There'll be a wonderful banquet for all royal guests, and speeches, and then the happy couple will lead us through a rose-petal arch and into the palace ballroom."

"That's right!" King Frank was still beaming with enthusiasm. "And Tertius has brought the Niven's Knowe musicians with him, so the music will be wonderful, and of course his sisters will be there, so *that's* a fine thing too!"

"Ah!" Marcus nodded. That explained why Arry was looking so horribly cheerful. Princess Nina-Rose was exceptionally pretty. She was also, in Marcus's opinion, exceptionally dull. Almost as dull as Tertius, in fact. *And* Princess Fedora. The whole bunch of them made the muddiest puddle positively sparkle in comparison.

"So make sure you get a good night's sleep, boys." King Frank rubbed his hands together and smiled proudly at his sons. "After all, who knows what other royal alliances might be made tomorrow in Dreghorn, eh? Eh?" And he nudged Arry.

"Exactly so, Father," Arry said, and blushed.

Marcus sighed, but quietly. "I'm *never* going to have

a crush on a girl," he promised himself. "It makes you look like a sick sheep."

"We go at ten sharp." King Frank slapped Arry on the back. "Make sure you're ready! And dressed in your best, of course." He winked at Marcus, who pretended not to notice. "Nina-Rose has lots of jolly little sisters, so best dress clothes for you, Marcus m'lad."

"Yes, Father," Marcus said as politely as he could. "May I go now? I've work to do for Professor Scallio." He bowed once more and scooted out of the throne room to the stable. If he hurried, he'd be in time to help Ger with the riding horses as well as the horses for the state coach, and he fully intended to stay for as long as he was needed. Maybe even longer.

Marcus whistled cheerfully as he swung into the stable yard. He was feeling very differently about those five hundred lines. If Professor Scallio was as good as his word—and he usually was—he might just be able to escape what promised to be the most boring outing ever. . . .

Chapter Six

As Gracie hurried along the path behind the flitting bat, she began to wonder if she was being very foolish. After all, what did she know about the bat and his plans for her? On the other hand, there was nothing about her life with Mange and Foyce that made her want to stay with them. It was only the house she was fond of. She'd been born there and had lived there happily enough until her father had died of Bluefoot Fever when she was two. Her mother had fallen ill a week or so later but had insisted on going to the market as usual. She had left Gracie with a neighbor and driven off with a cartload of onions. She had come back with Mange and Foyce and died shortly afterward. Mange had immediately claimed the house as his own, and there was nobody who dared to challenge him. He had told the neighbor that he had promised Gracie's mother he would care for Gracie, and as the neighbor had eleven children of her own, she was grateful not to have to add another to the collection. Gracie herself might have preferred to be one of a dozen underfed but happy children, but nobody asked her, and it wasn't long before Mange made himself so unpleasant that the neighbor moved away. Since then there had been no other neighbors, and Gracie had grown up believing that Mange was her stepfather. As she got older, she found it harder and harder to believe that her mother would have chosen to marry such a man, but after a lot of thought she had decided that her mother's fever must have affected her judgment.

Gracie sighed and shifted her knotted shawl to her other shoulder. When she thought of Mange, she knew that anything unknown *had* to be better than the known. All the same, it wouldn't hurt to ask some questions.

"Excuse me," she said as she and the bat passed the pile of boulders that marked the entrance to the village of Fracture and the path narrowed to a steep zigzag. "Excuse me, but do you have a name? Of course, if you don't want to tell me, that's quite OK, but—" Gracie stopped. The bat was behaving very oddly. He kept zooming high into the air and then dropping like a stone.

"Are you all right?" Gracie asked anxiously. "Is something wrong?"

The bat flew close to her ear. "Sure is, kiddo," he hissed. "We're being trailed. Got to think of a way to lose her."

"*Her?*" Gracie's heart began to race. "Oh, NO! It's not Foyce, is it? She'll kill me if she catches me. Is she close? She can run *much* faster than I can—"

"Not while she's stew-doped, she can't." The bat flew up, checked, and came back again. "Got ten minutes before she catches up, I'd say. Hey! Can you climb?"

"I can try," Gracie said.

"Right! Keep walking . . . and stamp in that sandy spot there. Yup. Footprint, see? Now, onto the grass . . . and double back here. Over the edge and down you go—fast as you can, but *no noise*, right?"

Gracie followed the bat's instructions to the letter. The footprint was sharp and clear, and as she got ready to swing herself off the path and onto the rocks below, she had another idea. She pulled off a shoe and threw it as hard as she could. It landed way down the path, far beyond the footprint.

The bat grinned. "Good thinking! Now, quick—before the dame gets around the corner and sees you. Straight down, and if I say *freeze*, then do it. Get it?"

"Got it." Gracie tucked the other shoe into her shawl and began scrambling down the precipitous rocks while the bat flew beside her, making encouraging squeaks. It was hard work, and more than once she slipped and skinned her elbows or knees, but she was getting down the steep mountainside far faster than if she had kept to the path. "When do we get to rest?" She panted as she stopped for a moment to catch her breath and push her hair out of her eyes.

"Soon enough, kiddo," the bat said. "See that crack in the rock there?"

Gracie looked. The crack was narrow and covered with bracken. If the bat hadn't pointed it out, she would have missed it altogether.

"Slip inside," the bat said. "If Uncle Alvin fusses, say Marlon sent you. I'll be along in five. Time to check out the dame. *Ciao!*" And before Gracie had time to argue, he was gone, flying up and away into the evening shadows. Gracie gripped her shawl more tightly and pushed her way into the darkness of the cave.

At first she could see nothing, but gradually her eyes

grew accustomed to the gloom. The space was far larger than had seemed possible from the narrow opening, and Gracie found herself wondering if it was more of a tunnel than a cave. She didn't want to explore, however. It reminded her much too clearly of the cellar where she had spent so many evenings, and she settled herself near the entrance to wait for the bat. Her back was against the rocky wall, and although it was anything but smooth, she felt her eyelids closing. . . .

"OI!"

The voice was sharp as a needle and right beside Gracie's ear. She woke up with a start and rubbed her eyes.

"Oi! What *exactly* do you think you're doing in *my* cave?"

"I'm so sorry," Gracie said, and then remembered the bat's instructions. "Erm . . . might you be Uncle Alvin?"

"I might," the voice said, and it did not sound any friendlier. "Or I might not. Who are you?"

"I'm Gracie Gillypot," Gracie said. "And I was to say that Marlon sent me and that he'll be along in five."

"Well, *that's* a load of rats' tails for a start," snapped the voice. "You've been here at least an hour. Unless that ridiculous nephew of mine meant five *hours*?"

"An *hour*?" Gracie felt a wave of panic surge through her. "I've been here a whole *hour*?"

"Well, I haven't been counting every minute," Uncle Alvin said. "I'm afraid I've had *far* more important things to do. But I'd say an hour at least. Maybe two."

Gracie clutched her bag to her chest. "But that's *awful*," she said, her voice wobbling. "What if he never comes back? What shall I do? I don't know where I'm going or *anything*. . . ."

Uncle Alvin sighed a small bat-size sigh. "Typical," he said. "Nothing but trouble, that boy. Always has been, and always will be. I mean, just *look* at the people he associates with! Witches, wizards, wizened old crones . . . and I've heard he even spends time with some waster in Gorebreath Palace! Huh!"

"Crones . . ." Gracie caught eagerly at the word. "I remember now! The bat—Marlon? Is that his name?—said he was taking me to the Ancient Crones." She shivered. "Although I don't know why."

Uncle Alvin didn't answer at once. When he did,

his voice sounded odd. "Ah. To the Ancient Crones. That might well be." He coughed as if he were embarrassed. "In that case, I apologize if I was a little—shall we say—cranky? when I woke you up." He coughed again. "And perhaps you'd be kind enough not to hold it against me, young lady, if we should ever have the good fortune to meet in the future."

"It's quite all right," Gracie said, wondering why he sounded so different all of a sudden. "It must be very inconvenient having humans blundering into your home. But I'll never get anywhere if Marlon doesn't come back to show me the—"

"La-di-da and la-di-deee—hello there, kiddo!" A tiny dark shape hung in the opening of the cave, and Marlon flipped inside. "See you met ol' misery guts!"

"He was being very kind," Gracie said reproachfully. "You were gone for *ages*!"

"Sorry 'bout that." Marlon didn't sound sorry at all. "Unavoidably delayed. Good news is, the dame's off track. Totally taken in by the shoe, if you ask my opinion. Heading toward Gorebreath, muttering and cursing all the way."

Gracie didn't ask what Foyce was muttering or whom she was cursing. She knew.

"So we'll be off as well," Marlon told her. "It'll be a bit of a trot, but you won't mind that, will you?"

Gracie shook her head. The very mention of Foyce had made her absolutely certain that she wanted to be anywhere Foyce wasn't. "Let's go," she said.

Uncle Alvin rustled his wings. "Off to the Ancient Crones, I hear," he said.

"Yup. Safest place when there's a dame on the rampage like the one out there." Gracie had a suspicion that Marlon was grinning. "Never heard swearing like it!"

"You be careful, my lad," Uncle Alvin said. "One of these days you're going to get yourself into such trouble, you won't find a way out, fast-talker though you may be. And don't forget that the Ancients hold the Power . . . far more than you could ever dream of."

"Yabber yabber yabber," Marlon said happily. "See you, Unc. Now, kiddo—off we go!" And he led Gracie out of the cave and into a bright moonlit night.

Chapter Seven

Gubble stared at the donkeys. He wasn't sure if he liked donkeys. He wasn't sure if donkeys liked him. He patted the biggest, and it bit him. Gubble was about to bite it back when Lady Lamorna came sweeping down the steps from the castle front door, a cloak wrapped closely around her. For a moment, Gubble didn't recognize his mistress. Her cloak was tattered and torn and covered in mud, and her long white hair was hidden under an ancient bonnet that appeared to be made of old cabbage leaves. Her face was covered in lines and wrinkles, and an evil-looking wart had appeared on the end of her nose. A tuft of white whiskers sprouted from her chin.

"Arf," Gubble said admiringly. "*Lovely,* Your Evilness. Gubble is most impressified."

"Good," said Lady Lamorna. She would have preferred something more attractive, but Aged Peasant was easy and used very little of her ever-decreasing stock of spell powder. "Now, where are our travel bags?"

Gubble blinked. "Bags?" he said. "No bags, Evilness. But Gubble has donkeys. Look!"

There was an unpleasant pause while Lady Lamorna looked at the donkeys. "Gubble," she said at last, her voice as cold as ice, "*why* have you acquired fifteen donkeys?"

Gubble shuffled his feet. Explaining that if two were good, then more must be better was quite beyond him. "Gold," he offered. "Lots of gold."

Lady Lamorna grew marginally less chilly. "Indeed, Gubble, it would be good to believe we will earn gold enough for fifteen donkeys. I suspect, however, that so many will slow us down. Besides, they will need feeding. Choose the two strongest while I return to the castle and pack my bag."

Gubble, mightily relieved at being let off so lightly, chose the strongest donkeys by the simple method of heaving himself onto their backs. Eight collapsed immediately, and Gubble tidied them away by dropping them over the castle battlements. They fell into the bushes beneath and galloped back to their homes, complaining bitterly. Of the seven that remained standing, five ran off as soon as Gubble had dismounted.

Gubble looked at the two remaining animals and saw that one was the donkey that had bitten him. "No more bitings," Gubble growled. "No biting or I bites your tail off. In fact, maybe I bite it now to teach you—"

"Gubble? My bag is ready!" Lady Lamorna was standing at the door. The donkey, saved for the second time that day, immediately developed a passionate attachment to Gubble's mistress. It trotted forward and brayed loudly before kneeling at her feet.

"Obviously an animal with sense," she remarked. "Gubble! Make sure this beast is treated well! I shall call it Figs, and I shall ride it myself."

The donkey gave Gubble a triumphant look. Gubble muttered darkly and strapped Lady Lamorna's bag onto the back of the second donkey before hauling himself into the saddle.

"Let us go!" Lady Lamorna waved her arm, and the party set off on the winding path that led down to the village of Fracture, and from there onward to Gorebreath.

Chapter Eight

To say that Foyce was angry would be an under-statement. To think that Gracie had escaped her, and—worse still—escaped with what was undoubt-edly some kind of magical help, made her blood boil. Her head was still fogged by the sleeping spell, but with every step, her mind was growing clearer. As she hurried along the path to Gorebreath, she ground her teeth and stamped her feet, and dreamed up more and more terrible ways of getting her revenge. "I'll boil her in her own magic soup," she promised her-self. "I'll make her work until her fingers are nothing but bone. I'll keep her in the cellar until she's green with mold—"

Foyce stopped. In front of her was a clear foot-print—the footprint of a small worn shoe. Foyce chuckled nastily, and within seconds she had found the shoe itself. She picked it up and turned it over. Yes! There was sand on the sole. Foyce frowned. She glanced back up the path. The footprint had been very clear. Too clear? And there was grass between the footprint and the shoe . . . surely the sand should have been rubbed from the sole?

If it hadn't been for the lingering effects of the Trueheart Stew, Foyce would have gone back and peered over the edge of the rocks—and if she had, she would have seen Gracie, and Gracie's fate would have been sealed. As it was, Foyce stood and considered it, then shook her muddled head.

"No," she decided. "No. The little worm isn't clever enough. She'd never think to play a trick like that! But she must be near—this shoe's still warm. I'll find her and catch her and twist her skinny little arms off!"

And Foyce flew on down the path and into the darkness of the forest that crouched around the base of Fracture Mountain. On and on she ran, until her breath grew ragged and she was finally forced to stop to rest. She found a twisted tree and leaned against it, panting.

"Where can the disgusting little slug be?" she wondered. "Surely I should have found her by now."

Foyce pulled the shoe from her pocket and smelled it. Then, after looking around to make sure there was nobody watching, she kneeled down to sniff the path.

When she stood up, her face was livid. *"She's not been this way at all!"* Foyce stomped a clump of buttercups into the ground with such force that they were churned into a muddy paste. "She's slipped away from the path! But *where?*"

And then, her mind now quite free from the spell, she remembered the footprint and the shoe, and she spat. "So she went down the rocks, did she? But she *must* be going to Gorebreath. There's nowhere else. So what I'll do is find her there . . . and won't I make her wish she'd stayed at home with me!" Foyce spat again.

She was about to walk on when she heard the faint jingle of a harness behind her. Immediately wary, she slipped behind the tree and into the gloom of the thick, tangled undergrowth, and she waited to see who was coming.

A witch?

Foyce stood very still as Lady Lamorna and Gubble trotted past her on their donkeys; she stared, taking in every detail. As they disappeared around a bend in the path, she moved quietly out of her hiding place and

followed, thinking hard. She had never heard of a witch in Fracture. But what else could the old hag be? It was true she had no pointed hat, but she smelled of evil. Foyce knew there was a sorceress who lived in the castle high above the village, and she had often thought fondly that they might appreciate each other's company, but a *witch*? Where could she have come from?

Foyce frowned and quickened her steps until she was near enough to see the back view of the two riders without being seen herself. As she came closer, she heard a cold clear voice ask the troll-like figure on the second donkey if he would hand her the map.

The troll gulped and shook his head. "No map, Your Evilness," he said.

The witch—if witch she was—snatched up her whip and began to beat her companion viciously. Foyce grinned as she watched him ducking and grunting beneath the blows. This was the kind of woman she understood, a woman after her own cold heart.

"Gubble will find the way!" the troll protested. "Gubble promises Your Evilness!"

"You must not call me that!" the witch snapped. "Remember that I am a poor, old peasant woman seeking an audience with the king. Or even better, the prince!"

Gubble perked up. "Prince!" he said. "Prince. *Zap!* Frog. Gubble remembers!"

The witch glared at him. "Gubble," she said coldly, "you are *not* to mention anything about princes and frogs ever again! Do you understand? And from now on, you had better call me something very ordinary, something that will never make people suspect us. Call me . . . call me Grandmother Bones."

Gubble nodded. "Whatever you says, Evilness— Ouch!"

Foyce drew in her breath as Gubble was slapped again. This was no witch. Neither was she a poor, old peasant woman. This was surely the sorceress from the castle, Lady Lamorna. But why was she in disguise? Foyce had never heard tell of the Lady leaving her castle before, so something extraordinary must be forcing her away. Something, by the sound of it, that involved princes and frogs. Foyce licked her lips. She had gifts that might well be useful to an unscrupulous and evil sorceress . . . and that would surely result in some kind of reward. A big reward.

Excellent! Foyce thought. *I shall find out what's going on and then see what I can do. We're all going the same way, so I can still deal with that slimy little toad Gracie Gillypot when I sniff her out.* And, keeping well in the shadows of the tall trees, she followed Lady Lamorna and Gubble to where the forest ended and the Kingdom of Gorebreath began.

The evening star was high and the night air very cold by the time they left the forest, and Foyce was glad to see Lady Lamorna order Gubble to stop outside a small roadside inn. He vanished inside but reappeared immediately with a large dog yapping at his heels and a burly innkeeper shouting at him to *"Get orf out of it and niver come back!"*

Lady Lamorna, evidently believing her disguise as an aged peasant was more than adequate, then tried to engage the innkeeper in conversation, with only moderate results. The innkeeper was deeply suspicious and not to be persuaded by the piece of gold he was offered. If anything, it made him more wary.

Foyce smiled with malicious satisfaction as she saw Lady Lamorna of Fracture Castle accepting an outhouse for her night's lodging, while Gubble and the donkeys took up residence in the ditch nearby. Once they were settled and Gubble was snoring loudly,

Foyce smoothed her tumbling blond curls and tiptoed past. Looking as she did, it was easy for her to charm her way into the very best bedroom and secure a free supper.

"What a *beeeeautiful* lady!" sighed the innkeeper's wife as she cut a generous portion of pie.

"Could be a princess in disguise," agreed the innkeeper. "But did you see that old bag who wanted a room? Where would the likes of her find a gold piece? She's a bad 'un, no mistake."

His wife nodded. "You'd best lock the outhouse door on her. We don't want her frightening the pretty lady. Or stealing our turnips. Or putting spells on the house in the night!"

"She can't be much good at spells," the innkeeper said, "or she'd have magicked up a much better place than ours!"

And they both roared with laughter as they hurried into the parlor to find the very best tablecloth for Foyce's benefit.

Chapter Nine

Prince Marcus was doing his best to look heartbroken as he ate his supper under his father's disapproving glare and his mother's reproachful gaze. He had spent a most enjoyable afternoon and evening helping Ger with the horses and had strolled back to the palace sometime after seven with hay in his hair and the whiff of the stable heavy on his clothes. He hadn't been entirely surprised to find Professor Scallio waiting for him on the front steps.

"Where, Prince Marcus, are the five hundred lines that I assigned to you as punishment?" his tutor inquired in frosty tones.

Marcus slapped his forehead and tried to look astonished and repentant at the same time. "Oh, no!" he gasped. "I'm *so* sorry. I forgot all about them! I'll do them as soon as I've washed up."

"You'll do no such thing," Professor Scallio told him. "I warned you. And I always mean what I say. Tomorrow you will stay here and complete your punishment while your family enjoys themselves in Dreghorn. I shall go and inform your father of my decision this very minute."

As the little tutor scuttled away, Marcus tried hard not to cheer and punch the air. A whole day to himself—*and* the evening too! He'd get the lines done first thing, and then he'd take his pony and go out exploring. . . .

Wow!

A sudden idea sent Marcus reeling across the driveway. Could he—*dare he*—leave the palace grounds? Could he get as far as the borders of Gorebreath and see what lay outside? The very thought made his heart beat wildly. There could be dragons, or bears, and all kinds of adventures. He had another idea. The *map*! Of course! He could take the map, and then there would be no danger of getting lost.

Tomorrow morning, as soon as his family had left, he'd head for the library, collect the map, and be off.

In the meantime he had to appear profoundly dejected.

"I cannot believe how irresponsible you have

been," the king said for the fourteenth time. "Not only have you treated your tutor with disrespect, but you've completely ignored his instructions!"

"And Princess Nina-Rose's sisters will be *so* disappointed not to see you," the queen said plaintively.

Marcus sighed, then ate his supper as slowly as he could, even though he was starving. When he had finished, he stood up and bowed. "Dear Father, dear Mother and Arry," he said. "I wish to apologize for my behavior, and I wish you the very best of days tomorrow. I shall now take myself to my bedroom, where I will spend at least an hour considering how badly I have let you all down."

The queen's eyes shone. "Oh, Marcus!" she said. "That is so *wonderful* of you!" She turned to the king. "Surely we could allow him to come tomorrow after all?"

Marcus's heart missed a beat. *Rats!* he thought. *I've overdone it. . . .*

But the king was still frowning. "I appreciate your apology, Marcus," he said, "but you must take your punishment like a true prince." He glanced at the queen. "Although . . . perhaps we might arrange another day of celebration for Princess Fedora's engagement here in Gorebreath?"

The queen clapped her hands and beamed. "Oh, *yes*!" she enthused. "What a *brilliant* idea, my dear! Isn't that a lovely idea, Marcus? And Arry—what do you think?"

"Fabulous idea, Father," Arry said, and he blushed.

The idea of yet another royal celebration made it much easier for Marcus to look depressed as he made his final bow and left the royal dining room.

At least I'll have a really good day tomorrow, he said to himself as he trudged up the stairs to his bedroom. *And I'll make sure I use every single second!* He flung himself across his bed and set his alarm clock for six. *I'll get those dratted lines done early, and then as soon as everyone's left for Dreghorn, I'll be off —and won't I have fun!*

Chapter Ten

Gracie Gillypot was wondering why she wasn't more tired. She had been following Marlon through the night for what seemed like ages and ages, but her feet weren't sore even though she was barefoot. She had no idea at all where she was; once they had reached the bottom of Fracture Mountain, they had turned sharply away from the path that led to Gorebreath and struck out into the dark heart of the forest. Marlon had led her between ancient gnarled and twisted trees and through wild tangled bushes, and although Gracie suspected that they were steadily moving west and climbing upward, she couldn't be certain.

The moon was beginning to fade and the birds beginning to sing happily about dawn and day and worms, when Marlon stopped under a wide-spreading yew tree. "OK, babe," he said. "Time for a nap. This bat's one tired flapper. Curl yourself up on a branch and snooze."

Gracie looked at the tree anxiously. She couldn't imagine how she could curl herself up on any branch.

Marlon yawned. "Climb, kiddo, climb. And no fretting. No one in this wood touches a Trueheart. See ya!" With a flip of his wings, he flew high into the branches and vanished.

There didn't seem to be any other choice, so Gracie climbed. To her surprise she found a deep hollow where a couple of large branches met the trunk, and the hollow was filled with soft, dry bracken. "This really is quite cozy," she murmured. "Although I'm sure I won't sleep. There's been far too much happening . . ." Her voice faded away, and her eyes closed. She began to snore faintly.

Marlon, perched several branches above her, chuckled. "Poor little kid. She needs a rest, and there's nothing like bracken dust to keep your peepers shut. Heigh-ho!" He shook himself, turned upside down, and batnapped for an hour. After that, he flew off on a little private business, but he was back before the sun was high in the sky.

Gracie woke with a start. For a moment she

couldn't imagine where she could possibly be, and then she remembered. She sat up in her nest of bracken and looked around. "How long have I slept?" she wondered aloud. And then, "Where's Marlon?"

"No worries. Don't think I'd bring you all this way to dump you, do you, kiddo?" Marlon was perched on the branch above, looking dusty but cheerful. "Ready to move?" he asked.

Gracie stretched. "Yes," she said. "Of course . . . but is there any chance I could wash my face and hands?" She was too polite to say she was starving.

"Overrated if you ask me," Marlon remarked. "Washing wears you away. But"—he waved a wing—"there's a stream down there if you must."

"Thank you," Gracie said gratefully, and she climbed down from her tree and hurried to the stream. Ten minutes later, as thoroughly washed as she could manage in a muddy trickle of water, she was back.

Marlon greeted her with a grin and pointed at a clump of stunted shrubs growing nearby. "Breakfast," he said. "Or whatever. Eat what you can, and save some. We'll be into the More Enchanted Forest before long. Don't trust anything there—not unless you're looking for shakes and shivers and a good deal worse."

Gracie helped herself to the small black berries doubtfully at first, but once she had tasted them, her face lit up. "Wow!" she said. "It's like . . . I don't know what it's like. It keeps changing! It's very delicious, though."

"Toast 'n' marmalade 'n' scrambled eggs 'n' bacon 'n' tomato 'n' porridge 'n' chips 'n' sauce," Marlon said, all in one breath.

"Oh." Gracie was impressed. "Is that what it is? I think Foyce and Mange must have eaten those things when they went to Gorebreath market. I recognize the names."

Marlon stared at her. "You don't say. And what did you get, kiddo?"

Gracie swallowed another handful of berries. "They always left me behind, locked in the cellar. And I ate potato peelings, mostly. Or porridge skin."

"Porridge skin. Ah." Marlon turned his back on Gracie, and she had a sudden suspicion that he was wiping his eyes with his wing. He looked his normal chirpy self when he turned back, however, and she decided she must have been mistaken. "OK, babe!" he said. "Picked enough berries to keep you going? Time we left. Can't keep the Ancient Crones waiting.

This way!" And he flitted away along a pathway totally invisible to Gracie's human eye.

Gracie followed obediently, but as she jumped over the small stream, Marlon's words echoed in her head. What did he mean, keep the Ancient Crones waiting? Did they know she was coming? And if so, how? She pushed away a trailing creeper and scrambled noisily over a heap of slithering stones. Several fell away from under her feet and rattled to the bottom of a slope. "Marlon!" she called. "Marlon!"

Marlon flew a loop over her head and twittered crossly. "Shhh!" he hissed. "No need to tell the whole forest we're here! News'll get around quick enough as it is."

"I'm sorry," Gracie whispered. "But I was wondering—why are the Ancient Crones waiting for me?"

"What?" Marlon looped another loop. "When did I say that?"

"You said we mustn't keep them waiting," Gracie said doggedly.

"Did I?" Marlon sounded shifty. "Just a turn of phrase, kiddo. Don't you go thinking up stories, now. Just trust your old friend Marlon!" And he was off again, this time flying well in front of her.

He doesn't want to talk about it, Gracie thought, and then she shrugged. *But I'm going to have to trust him. I don't know where I am or where I'm going, except that it's to the Ancient Crones . . . and however scary and peculiar they may be, absolutely* anything *is better than Mange and Foyce.*

Chapter Eleven

Lady Lamorna woke early thinking of deeply unpleasant things to do to the innkeeper and his wife. When she had tried to open the outhouse door in the night, she had found it locked, and this had not improved her temper. "Gubble!" she called. "Gubble!"

Gubble was happily asleep in his ditch with his head on his donkey and didn't hear her.

Lady Lamorna cursed fluently and pulled a small spell from the battered leather pouch she had tied to her belt before leaving the castle. "What a waste," she muttered. "I was saving this for a time when it was really needed!" She blew a small puff of powder onto the lock, and the door opened easily. Lady Lamorna stormed out and pulled Gubble's nose as hard as she could.

Gubble woke up, shouting and waving his arms, and the donkey got frightened and began to bray loudly.

"Silence!" shrieked Lady Lamorna. "Silence!" And she flicked the donkey on the nose. At once it was quiet, but it was too late. The innkeeper and his wife and the dog were hurrying toward them, the innkeeper brandishing a fearsome pitchfork and his wife waving a rolling pin.

Lady Lamorna hesitated. All her instincts were to turn the innkeeper and his wife and his dog into stone, but even though she was incandescent with anger, she knew that would be a mistake. Not only would awkward questions be asked when they were found, but more important, it would use up a large reserve of her powers.

She made a decision. "Hurry!" she shouted, and grabbing Figs by the bridle, she vaulted onto its back and kicked it sharply. Figs immediately broke into a shambling gallop, and the innkeeper, his wife, and their dog were left to face Gubble. His night in the ditch had made him extremely muddy, and the pulling of his nose had made him extremely cross. Cross enough to forget that he usually gave all dogs a wide berth. He scowled heavily. "I bites," he told the dog. "I bites *hard*!"

The dog whimpered, turned tail, and fled.

Gubble grinned a mirthless and toothless grin and took a step forward. "That's what I does," he growled at the innkeeper. "I bites *HARD!*"

The innkeeper lowered his pitchfork and looked nervously at Gubble, then at his wife.

His wife dropped her rolling pin and took her husband's arm. "Norbottle," she said, "come back to the inn this minute. Don't you go forgetting we've got a pretty young lady to look after! We've no time for riff-raff like this!"

And the two of them hurried away, leaving Gubble feeling marginally better. He hauled his donkey out of the ditch and set off after Lady Lamorna as fast as he could.

Foyce, peeping from behind the lacy curtains of the inn's best bedroom, had seen everything that had happened. She had even seen the puff of purplish smoke floating from the outhouse door before Lady Lamorna had come out. She had also noticed the expression of thwarted fury on Lady Lamorna's face as she had ridden away.

"Things aren't going right for her," Foyce told herself, and smiled at her own enchanting reflection in the mirror. "All the better for me!" And she took herself downstairs for a delicious breakfast of lightly boiled eggs and toast. After she had eaten all she could, which was a surprising amount for such a slender young woman, she explained to the hovering innkeeper that she had no money to pay for her night's lodging. She fluttered her long, long eyelashes as she spoke, and Norbottle was more than happy to cancel her debt in exchange for a kiss. His wife snorted but did not protest. There was something about Foyce that was making her uncomfortable. The young woman was just as pretty as she'd been the night before, she thought, but when you looked at her eyes, it made your bones go icy cold.

Foyce walked away feeling that life was good, while Norbottle rubbed at his cheek. It was red and inflamed, and as the day went on, it began to itch unbearably.

Chapter Twelve

On the same morning, Prince Arioso of Gorebreath and his twin brother, Prince Marcus, also got up early. Arry wanted to have plenty of time to get dressed in his finest clothes. Marcus wanted to get his lines written before his family went off to Dreghorn.

"Goodness, Marcus!" Arry said in amazement as he watched his brother scratching away with his quill as if his life depended on it. "If you keep writing at that speed, you'll be finished in time to come with us after all!"

Marcus hastily crossed out the last ten lines and dropped his quill nib down on the wooden floor. "Bother," he said as convincingly as he was able. "Now I'll have to go and find a new one!"

"Oh, bad luck!" Arry said. "Here, would you like mine? Shall I sharpen it for you?"

"That's very kind," Marcus said, "but I'm sure to spoil it. I'll fetch one from the library later. Don't worry about me—just get yourself ready to go. Look, I'll fetch your shoes for you *and* your coat!"

"Goodness, Marcus!" Arry opened his eyes wide. "I really think I should ask Mother—"

"Don't!" Marcus said, and bundled Arry into his waistcoat.

Despite Marcus's efforts to rush his brother, it seemed hours and hours before the coaches finally rolled away down the long drive. Right up until the last moment, Arry had been helpfully suggesting that Marcus might still be allowed to come to the party, and Marcus was all but worn out with the effort of avoiding such a dreadful fate. But now, at last, they were gone. He waved a final good-bye, then sprinted up the stairs to the royal library.

He crashed through the doors and slid across the polished wooden floor—and came face to face with Professor Scallio. "Oh," Marcus said blankly. "I mean, good morning, sir."

"You mean," the professor said blandly, "you weren't expecting to see me here."

"Erm . . . no. Th-that is," Marcus stammered, "I thought you'd gone with the others to Dreghorn. . . ."

"And leave one of my pupils all alone? I think not." Professor Scallio adjusted his spectacles. "Have you finished your lines?"

"Yes!" Marcus dug inside the pocket of his trousers. "Here you are!" And he handed over the crumpled sheets of paper.

"Thank you so much," the professor said. "Perhaps I might give you this in return?" And he picked up a roll of cracked and discolored parchment from his desk and handed it to Marcus. "This was what you were coming to collect, was it not?"

Marcus's mouth opened and shut several times, but he was quite unable to speak.

"Prince Marcus!" His tutor frowned. "Kindly do *not* display the characteristics of a goldfish! Surely you did not think I was unaware of your interest in this item?"

"Erm . . . yes, sir. That is . . . no, sir." Marcus felt he was not doing well. "That is—I mean, thank you *very* much, sir!"

Professor Scallio nodded and began to move away. "Just remember," he said over his shoulder, "that this meeting between us has never taken place." And he wandered off into the darkest recesses of the library.

"No—that is, yes, sir . . ." Marcus shook his head. He wasn't sure if he was dreaming, but the map crackled invitingly in his hand, and he let out a whoop of joy. "Thank you!" he called into the darkness, and rushed out of the library and down the stairs.

Pausing only to grab his jacket, he hurried to the stable to find Ger already leading his pony out into the yard.

"Ger, you are my best friend *ever!*" Marcus said, and swung himself into the saddle.

"Are you sure you ain't wanting me to come with you, Your Highness?" Ger asked a little anxiously. He knew enough of Marcus's plans to feel concerned for him.

Marcus would very much have liked Ger to come too, but he also knew that Ger had plans to spend the day with Daisy, the youngest and prettiest palace cook. "It's OK, Ger," he said. "I'll be careful—and I promise that if I get eaten by bears, I'll get the bears to tell my father that I saddled Glee myself."

Ger grinned. "D'you still want my coat?"

"If that's OK," Marcus said.

Ger pulled a grubby old jacket from a nail on the wall, and the two boys ceremoniously swapped garments.

"Daisy'll like this," Ger said, looking down at the blue velvet and golden buttons. "You have fun, now!" And he went out of the yard whistling.

Chapter Thirteen

Marcus took a deep breath. This was the moment when his adventure would begin. He had the map safely in his pocket and now there was nothing to stop him. He clucked gently to Glee and rode steadily out of the stable yard and around to the front of the Royal Palace. As he trotted down the long poplar-lined drive, he could see a most unusual flurry of activity outside the lodge gates. Half of him was tempted to cut across the pristine green lawns and head for the fence, but the other half was consumed with curiosity. The curiosity won, and Marcus kicked Glee into a canter and headed for the lodge. As he drew closer, he could see the guards gathered threateningly around a bent old woman, two donkeys, and what looked suspiciously like a troll. They were, without doubt, Persons of *Extremely* Dubious Respectability.

"This really is the best day *ever*," Marcus said to himself, and he rode Glee behind the lodge. He threw the pony's reins over a railing, slid from the saddle, and crept around the side wall.

"I *demand* to see the king!" The voice was high and imperious. "I am a poor, unfortunate peasant woman. My name is Grandmother Bones, and I *must* see him!"

Marcus had seen many peasant women, but never one like this. She had unbent now, and he could see that she was even taller than his father. As her eyes flashed, shivers crawled down his spine. "Nasty," he said to himself. "*Very* nasty!"

"Excuse *me*, madam, but the king ain't here today," the captain of guards was explaining in testy tones. "I've told you ten times already, madam, and I'd be grateful if you'd just be off."

The troll half hopped, half staggered forward. "I bites," he growled. "I bites *hard!*"

"Be *silent*, Gubble," Grandmother Bones told him. "This is a time for diplomacy, not force." She leaned toward the captain, and her silver eyes held his in a hypnotic gaze as a tiny puff of purple smoke floated in the air between them. "Tell me this," she said. "If the king is not here, where can the prince be found?"

The captain blinked, gulped, and visibly shrank. "He's gone to Dreghorn, if you please, ma'am." He spoke in a monotone. "He's gone to Princess Fedora's engagement party, ma'am. They've all gone, ma'am, Crown Prince Arioso and the king and the queen— they went off not so long ago, ma'am—and only Professor Scallio—"

"Enough!" snapped Grandmother Bones. "I have no need to hear about servants! When do they return?"

The captain of guards wiped his hand over his red and sweaty face as if he were waking from a deep sleep. "What? What was that?"

Grandmother Bones repeated her question with increasing irritation. The captain rubbed his eyes, then stood up straight, folded his arms, and frowned. "Now then, old woman," he said briskly. "Enough's enough. I've answered your questions. The king ain't back until late tonight, and that's that, so off with you. The likes of you aren't welcome around here!"

For a moment Marcus thought that Grandmother Bones was going to strike the captain, but she drew back. "So I will find Prince Arioso at the Palace of Dreghorn," she said thoughtfully. "And many other princes and princesses will, no doubt, be there as well! Gubble, we must hurry!" She swung herself onto the larger of the donkeys and galloped away. Gubble, managing at last to struggle across his saddle, followed.

The guards watched them go, the captain shaking his head. "Never did see anything like that before," he said.

One of the younger guards coughed. "Erm . . . Do you think it was wise to tell that old bag where the Royal Fambly is, sir? I mean, she didn't look the friendly type to me. Nor that 'orrible troll."

"I never told her nothing!" the captain said indignantly. "Not a word! What do you take me for? If you've nothing better to do than make up stories, young Jim, you can make us all a good strong cup of tea! Talking to that old lady's left a nasty taste in my mouth." And he marched inside the lodge house, leaving the guards looking at one another in bewilderment.

"It'll be all right, Jimmy," a bewhiskered one said reassuringly. "They'll have soldiers and guards everywhere at Dreghorn Palace. And if she comes back here tomorrow, you can run up to the palace and warn 'Is Majesty, double quick. Now, let's have that cup of tea."

Marcus leaned against the wall to wait until the guards had disappeared. He was doing some serious thinking. Was Arry in danger? Should he abandon his plans and ride to Dreghorn? But what, after all, could he tell them? A weird-looking old woman and a mud-covered troll had been asking to see them. . . . Marcus frowned. He couldn't see his father considering either to be much of a threat. Trolls were unusual, to be sure, but not entirely unknown. And while there was something deeply unpleasant about Granny Bones, he had no proof she wanted anything other than an autograph . . . or whatever else it was that ancient old women hoped for from kings. And the guard had been right. Dreghorn had quite enough security to deal with most problems, and there was a delightful rose-covered jail in the center of the high street. But, then again, there had been that strange little puff of purple smoke. . . .

Marcus groaned in perplexity. "What do you think, Glee?" he asked his pony.

Glee whickered and pushed gently at Marcus's shoulder.

"That's no help," Marcus said. "Bother it all. I think

we're going to have to go to Dreghorn. I can't risk it—oh!" He suddenly brightened. "I know! I'll go and ask Professor Scallio what he thinks! Come on, Glee—with any luck, we'll be off to the mountains yet!"

Chapter Fourteen

As Marcus galloped up the driveway one way, Lady Lamorna and Gubble galloped in the other direction, Lady Lamorna muttering to herself. "Once I have those princes in my power, I'll teach their servants how to speak to me! I'll make them pay! Oh, *how* I'll make them pay! I'll make them pay double and triple times over . . . *Gubble!*"

"Yes, Evilness?" Gubble's voice was muffled. He was hugging his donkey's neck in an increasingly hopeless attempt to stay on its back.

"Which way should we go?" Lady Lamorna reined in Figs and stared at the crossroads ahead. She recognized the road that led back to Gorebreath village, but there was no signpost to suggest which of the three other roads led to Dreghorn.

"Umph," Gubble said, and fell off. His donkey brayed triumphantly and hurried away as fast as its legs would carry it.

Lady Lamorna glared down at her companion. Things were not going according to plan in any way, shape, or form, and she was angry. Angrier than she had been for a long, long time. "Gubble!" she spat. "Stand up!"

Gubble got up slowly, his thumb in his toothless mouth and terror in his piggy little eyes.

"Gubble!" his mistress hissed. "You are completely *useless!*" She slapped him as hard as she could. His head spun off, rolled across the dusty road, and came to rest in a clump of nettles. "Ow! Ow! Ow!" the head howled, and Lady Lamorna smiled in sour satisfaction.

"That'll teach you," she snarled, and then stopped. And stared. The most beautiful girl she had ever seen was walking down the road toward her, Gubble's donkey drooping beside her.

"I think this might belong to you, dear Mrs. Bones," said the girl as she tossed back her tumbling golden curls and smiled with her rosebud mouth. "May I introduce myself? My name is Foyce Undershaft, and there are things we need to talk about."

Lady Lamorna looked at Foyce suspiciously. "I thank you for returning the animal," she said, "but I see no reason for us to speak further. Unless, of course, you are expecting some kind of reward." She began to reach for her purse, but Foyce shook her head and smiled again. Lady Lamorna's experience of human beings was limited, but she did know that smiles were meant to be warm and friendly. She was interested to see that Foyce's smile was as friendly as the stare of a rattlesnake.

"Why don't we have a little get-together," Foyce suggested sweetly, but with the sweetness of poisonous berries. "Then we can chat more comfortably."

Foyce left the donkey standing in the middle of the road, its head hanging, and stepped into the stinging nettles. Lady Lamorna noticed that they had no effect on Foyce's delicate white skin, and her eyebrows rose. They rose even higher when she saw Foyce pick up Gubble's head without a shudder and tuck it neatly under the owner's arm.

As Gubble put himself back together, Foyce leaned against the dejected donkey. "I understand you have a plan," she said, and put a delicate finger to her rosy lips. "I do assure you that I'm the soul of discretion.

You mustn't think I've mentioned your arrival here in Gorebreath to *anyone*." She looked up and down the empty road and bobbed a little curtsy. "Of course," she whispered, "I do understand that you're traveling in disguise."

Lady Lamorna was, for once in her life, taken aback. Who was this girl? She was certainly different. There was no sickly stench of the milk of human kindness hanging around her. She took decapitation in her stride. Nettles didn't sting her. The overconfident donkey was in a state of piteous dejection. There was no doubt that she was evil . . . but evil, by its very nature, could not be trusted. Lady Lamorna decided to be careful. Very careful.

"Thank you for your interest, my dear," she said. "And I can see that you are a very clever girl, but I think I shall deal with my own business in my own way. Thank you again for stopping the donkey." Her tone changed. "Gubble! Get back in that saddle *now*!"

Foyce watched Gubble flailing about with a curious expression on her face. When he was ready to go, she curtsied again to Lady Lamorna. "We shall meet again, Your Evilness," she said smoothly, and was pleased to see the sorceress start. "Our ways are destined to join. Oh, the road to Dreghorn is the middle one—and I wish you a fine journey. I also hope you find as many princes as you need for your . . . for your business." She smiled her snake-like smile and sank down among the nettles to watch Lady Lamorna and Gubble riding away at a brisk trot.

Chapter Fifteen

Professor Scallio listened intently as Marcus described the strange woman who had called herself Grandmother Bones and the squat, mud-covered, green-faced troll. When Marcus mentioned the little puff of purple smoke, the professor grunted and got up from his chair to fetch an old red leather-bound book from a pile on the floor.

Marcus, who had been hoping his tutor would pooh-pooh the whole event, thus setting him free for the rest of the day, felt increasingly worried. "Is it bad?" he asked.

Professor Scallio tapped the open book with his pencil. "Yes," he said. "I think it is."

Marcus leaped to his feet. "I must go to Dreghorn!" he exclaimed.

The tutor shook his head. "I fear," he said, "that it would be of little use."

"Why?" Marcus asked. "Glee can go like the wind—I can be there in plenty of time to warn them!"

"If you do that," Professor Scallio said slowly, "you might make things worse." He pushed the book forward, and Marcus saw a picture of a vial of purple powder. "Was the smoke you saw that color?"

Marcus nodded.

"Then," the tutor said, "I think we are almost certainly dealing with a sorceress. Most probably Lady Lamorna." He saw Marcus's eyes widen and asked, "Have you never wondered why your father was so set on you and Arioso staying within the Northern Plains? Why you have never been allowed to study the areas that lie outside the royal boundaries?"

Marcus looked blank. "I suppose I thought Father wanted us to know about local stuff because Arry'll be king of it all one day. I thought he just wasn't bothered about what went on outside. . . ."

"No, Prince Marcus," Professor Scallio said. "Your father didn't want you to know about the outside world because he is frightened. Not frightened for himself, you understand, but frightened that once you had heard about the Less Enchanted Wood, and the Wild Enchanted Forest, and the ancient sorceress of Fracture Castle, and the House of the Ancient Crones,

you would want to ride out and investigate."

"You *bet* I would!" Marcus agreed enthusiastically. "I was going to—that is—I mean . . ." He blushed bright red and began to stammer.

"You were going to ride out and explore today," said the tutor. "I know. That is why I gave you the map. It would have given you fair warning when you were near danger."

Marcus looked puzzled. "But you didn't try to stop me. . . ."

Professor Scallio sighed. "Your father and I disagree," he said. "I believe it is better to know what is there, so that you are aware of the dangers and can avoid them. Your father believes that if you ignore danger and keep it outside your door, it will go away, or at least not bother you." He sighed again. "But now it seems that danger has crossed right over the step and into the kingdom, and we must wait and see what it has in mind."

"Can't we just have the sorceress—what did you call her? Lady Moaner?—thrown into Dreghorn jail? And that troll as well?" Marcus wanted to know.

"But as yet they have done nothing wrong," Professor Scallio said. "And Dreghorn, like Gorebreath, is a democratic kingdom. There would be an uprising if anyone or anything was imprisoned without fair trial. No. I fear all we can do is keep our eyes wide open and wait. At least she has lost the advantage of complete surprise."

"I suppose so." Marcus got to his feet and began to wander idly around, inspecting the rows of gilt-framed pictures and the heavily laden bookshelves. Although Professor Scallio had been at the palace for more than seven years, Marcus had never seen his private rooms. The tutor had made it very clear that visitors were not welcome, but by the time Marcus had ridden back from the guardhouse, he had persuaded himself that Arry was in such deadly danger that he had flung himself into the tutor's sitting room without so much as a knock on the door. Now his eye was caught by the portrait of a small dumpy woman who looked remarkably like the professor, and he paused in front of it. "Is that your sister, sir? Are you twins?"

"How very observant of you, Prince Marcus," the tutor said. "I have been told that the likeness is extreme. But"—he neatly edged Marcus toward the door—"surely you are wanting to take your pony and make the most of your free day?" He saw Marcus's look of doubt. "I do promise you, dear boy, that your brother and family will come to no more harm without you than they would if you were there." He pushed

Marcus gently out onto the landing. "Just two words of advice. One—always keep the map close beside you. Two—in the most unlikely event of everything going seriously wrong, go to the House of the Ancient Crones. They know all the answers. Although"—the tutor stood back and eyed Marcus with a thoughtful look—"you do have the distinct disadvantage of being a boy. Still, they might stretch a point." After which cryptic remark Professor Scallio went back into his room, closing the door firmly behind him.

Marcus, left standing outside, dithered. He wasn't sure if he felt like adventuring now . . . but when would he ever have a free day again? He walked slowly down the staircase, thinking all the way. Glee whickered cheerfully to see him come out into the sunshine, and Marcus grinned.

"Hello, boy!" he said. "It's all right—we're going out after all. I've decided. We'll go to Dreghorn, but we won't let anyone see us. We'll go over the field and through the wood, and when we get there, I'll sneak up the old church tower. . . . I bet you can see right into the palace grounds from the top. I'll soon spot that old sorceress if she turns up with her horrible troll, and if anything looks suspicious, I'll ring the church bells until I burst!"

Chapter Sixteen

Gracie ate the last of her berries and licked her fingers. "I'm ready," she said, without much enthusiasm. "Are we nearly there?"

"Kiddo," Marlon said, "we'll be there when we're there."

Gracie sighed and got up from her seat on top of an exceedingly hard rock. She was aching all over and horribly thirsty. The berries were delicious but did nothing to quench her thirst. It was a long, long time since she and Marlon had left the yew tree and the little stream. "Couldn't we find another stream?" she asked.

Marlon groaned. "It'd take us way out of our way," he said. "Do y'like tea? Mugs and mugs of tea?"

"Oh, *yes*," Gracie said. "Yes, *please!*"

"Well, you'll have enough tea to float a boat just as soon as you get through the door," Marlon promised.

"Now, shake a leg. See the top of that hill? Over that, and we're snug as a bug in a rug."

"That's what you said when we came to the last hill," Gracie said. "And the hill before. And the hill before that."

"Had to keep your spirits up, kiddo," Marlon said unapologetically. "But this one's the one. Bona fide. Bat's honor. Now, off we go!"

To Gracie's amazement, Marlon was right. As she clambered wearily over the top, she saw a clearing in the thick forest below. A chaotic house was dropped into the middle. It looked as if it had once been a sensible sort of building, but someone had come along and muddled it all up: chimneys poked out of walls, the roof was peppered with cracked and dusty windows, the front door appeared to be balanced on top of an outhouse, and the front path jiggled and squiggled around and around the outside like a quite impenetrable maze. A misty haze hung low over the house, reaching to the very edges of the clearing.

"Can you see it, kiddo? Can you see it?" Marlon asked.

"Of course I can," Gracie said. "Erm . . . it doesn't look very . . . ordinary. There's an awful lot of green smoke."

"Knew you were a Trueheart," Marlon said. "If you weren't, you'd see nothing but forest. Smoke keeps prying eyes away, see."

Gracie pushed her hair back from her face and squinted more closely at the house below. "The path keeps changing direction," she said.

"Does it?" Marlon sounded surprised.

Gracie stared at him. "Can't you see it? Look! It keeps twisting all over the place. Now it's tied itself up in a bow!"

"I always fly in," Marlon said. "No need for paths. Come on, babe—got to get in before it gets too bright out here." And he zigzagged off ahead.

Gracie stumbled after him. As she traveled lower and lower, the trees grew thicker and the shrubby undergrowth was harder and harder to push through. Brambles caught her dress and pulled her hair, loops of grass tripped her, and small whippy branches flicked her as she passed. "I don't think anything here likes me much," she panted.

Marlon laughed. "You should see what happens to the Falsehearts, kiddo! There are bogs, and sinking sands, and all sorts of things!"

Gracie supposed she should be grateful, but as a

shower of wet and soggy leaves soaked her the very next moment, she decided she wasn't.

"Here we are!" Marlon flew a victory roll over Gracie's head. "See the gateway? Just over there?"

Gracie peered through the branches and found that there were two towering gateposts only a yard or two in front of her. In between was a ramshackle gate that couldn't make up its mind if it was open or closed. As Gracie watched, it opened wide, shut, quivered, opened a couple of inches, closed, and opened wide once more.

"Watch how you go through," Marlon warned. "For a magical gate, it ain't that clever."

Gracie pushed her way out from the sheltering trees, and the gate immediately slammed shut.

"Talk to it, kiddo," Marlon told her.

Gracie coughed politely and said, "Please, dear gate, may I come in?"

There was a long pause before the gate reluctantly creaked open just wide enough for Gracie to slide through. At once the path untangled itself and came zooming toward her, quivering like an excited puppy.

Marlon, high above Gracie's head, said, "See? It's pleased to see you. Be good, now, and I'll be back soon. Just remember to trust your old friend Marlon. . . ."

To Gracie's utter horror, he flapped his wings and vanished into the darkness of the forest. "Marlon!" she yelled, pulling at the gate to chase after him—but the gate wouldn't budge. Instead, the path tickled her ankles and rippled encouragingly.

Gracie tried hard not to cry. She fished in her pocket for a hankie, but all she could find was the soft little cloth that had contained her Trueheart Stew. She stuffed it back and wiped her nose on the edge of her shawl.

"You can't go back, Gracie Gillypot," she told herself firmly, "so you'll just have to go forward!" And to the path's great excitement, she strode out along it to see where it took her.

Chapter Seventeen

The road between Gorebreath and Dreghorn was longer than Lady Lamorna had expected, and it was well past midday by the time she crossed the border. She kept Figs moving at a brisk trot, and as Gubble fell off his donkey with increasing regularity, she reached the gates of the Royal Palace well ahead of him. To her extreme surprise and annoyance, she saw that Foyce Undershaft was there before her. Foyce was sitting on the knee of one soldier and smiling sweetly into the adoring eyes of another. Lady Lamorna would have been even more annoyed had she been able to hear what Foyce was saying.

"*Such* a big, muddy green-faced troll," she was lisping. "And it chased me all the way from Gorebreath! But now I know I'm safe, because you brave soldiers would *never* let such a horrid thing near the dear Royal Family, would you?"

"Never!" promised the soldiers. "Never ever!"

"Thank you," Foyce whispered coyly. Her business done, she jumped up and ran to meet the old sorceress. "Why, Granny Bones!" she called in her silvery voice. "How *lovely* to see you! Are you coming to the royal party? Shall we go together?" And she skipped toward Lady Lamorna in a cute and girlish way.

The soldiers at the gates immediately fell even more deeply in love with her, but Lady Lamorna could see the calculating look in Foyce's big blue eyes.

You don't fool me with that act of yours, she thought, and was about to brush Foyce to one side and ride through the gates when there was the clatter of galloping hooves and Gubble appeared in a cloud of dust.

"Help me, Evilness—help me!" he yelled—and flew past the gates, on down the road, and out of sight.

The soldiers immediately leaped to attention and swung the gates shut with a mighty clang. "Full alert!" barked the colonel-in-charge. " 'Ten*shun*! Troll sighted!"

Foyce watched the closing gates with a cool smile

and turned to the furious and frustrated Lady Lamorna. "I would have thought such an important person as yourself would have had a servant with— shall we say—more skills than a mere troll?" Foyce said. "Might I offer my services? I think you might find me very . . . useful." When she received no answer, Foyce twirled her fingers into Figs's mane. At once the donkey moaned and shivered.

Lady Lamorna had been secretly reaching for her leather purse, but now she paused to stare thoughtfully at Foyce. "And why might that be?" she asked.

"I have a way with animals," Foyce said sweetly. "And"—she indicated the soldiers, who were marching up and down behind the gates with a great deal of impressive foot stomping—"with men. But I don't wish to inconvenience Your Evilness. I want to benefit us both." And she led the quivering Figs to the far side of the road, where there was a comfortable bench provided for the aged of Dreghorn on their way back from market.

Lady Lamorna dismounted and sat down, her mind whirling. She was uncomfortably aware that her disguise had not been a success. Perhaps she was getting old and did need help. Human beings were so much more trouble than she remembered. Had it not been for her urgent need for gold, and plenty of it, she would happily have retreated to her castle that very moment . . . but her dress was ordered! And the Ancient Crones might take terrible revenge if she failed to pay her debts. Besides, she wanted that dress badly. *Very* badly.

Lady Lamorna looked slyly at Foyce. Could they work together? The girl certainly seemed able to charm her way wherever she wanted. But could she be trusted?

Foyce knew exactly what Lady Lamorna was thinking. She could smell her weariness and greed and suspicion, and she gave a tinkling laugh. "Trust is always such a problem, isn't it? Let me tell you what I know about you, and then I will tell you something about me that no one else knows." She paused. "You can use it against me if you need to."

Lady Lamorna leaned back against the bench. This girl was even cleverer than she had thought. "Go on," she said.

Foyce ticked off the points on her fingers as she spoke. "*One:* you are looking for princes. That is why you are here for the Royal Engagement Celebration. *Two:* you have plans for these princes. In the words of your green-faced servant: 'Prince. *Zap!* Frog.'

Three"—and here Foyce was hoping that her beautiful mask of a face gave no sign that she was guessing— "as your disguise is distinctly unoriginal, it follows that you are short of cash, so you are intending to use those frogs in order to bargain for a large reward. Gold." She laughed again. "I'm very fond of gold myself."

"You may be right," Lady Lamorna said, "or you may not. Tell me your secret."

Foyce twirled a ringlet and swung her dainty foot. "My mother was a werewolf. In Gorebreath, Dreghorn, and all the kingdoms of the Northern Plains, such an inheritance is punished with banishment. That is why my beloved father took me to live in Fracture. But now my time has come, dear Lady Lamorna. I can smell your excitement. Tell me the rest of your plan!"

Lady Lamorna made up her mind. She took a deep breath and leaned forward. "Listen," she said.

Chapter Eighteen

Marcus swung himself out of the saddle. The pony was hot and panting, and Marcus took time to walk him to and fro to cool him.

"Good boy," he said, "you did really well!" Then, leaving Glee to crop the long green grass in Dreghorn churchyard, he slipped into the doorway of the tall church tower and began to climb the steep stone steps. Up and up he climbed, the darkness only occasionally broken by a narrow shaft of light from a slitted window. Marcus tried hard not to think about what might be hiding in the gloom; it wasn't so much the darkness he minded as the thought that he could be trapped at the top of a solid stone spiral staircase. He breathed a sigh of relief as he came out onto the dusty balcony where the bells were hung. Gritting his teeth, he headed for the wooden ladder that led to a small door that led to the top of the tower.

Once Marcus was outside in the sunshine, all his fears fell away. He hurried to the edge and, as he had hoped, found he had a perfect view of the Royal Gardens. Anxiously he scanned the crowds and almost immediately saw Arry walking hand in hand with Princess Nina-Rose, while his parents beamed benevolently from behind.

"Phew," Marcus sighed. "So *that's* all right!"

"You reckon, kiddo? Keep watching. Look out for a dame with a great big basket!"

Marcus jumped, his heart flip-flopping so wildly in his chest that he couldn't speak.

"Keep your hair on," said the small squeaky voice. "And keep your peepers open. Action's just about to start, if you ask me. Which you ain't, but you should."

Marcus, having looked in all directions but the right one, finally found the owner of the voice crouched in the shadow of the weather vane. "Are you . . . are you a *bat*?" he asked in disbelieving tones.

"Sure am, kiddo. Not usually out in this weather. Can't see too good, so you keep looking." The bat waved a scaly wing. "D'you see the dame yet?"

Marcus obediently went back to the tower wall. "What sort of dame?"

A horrible thought leaped into his head. "You don't mean the tall one with whiskers? The one with the troll?"

"Nah—they wouldn't let her in." The bat chuckled. "She was outside the gates last I saw. Spitting mad. And the troll was all over the place—head one side of the road, body the other."

Marcus squinted into the sunlight, but the gates were too far away for him to make out anything very clearly. "So who am I looking for, then?"

"Told ya. Big basket."

"I can see lots of people with baskets," Marcus reported. "They're giving out ribbons and biscuits and flowers and stuff."

"Blond," the bat said. "Skippy. Big blue eyes."

"Oh!" Marcus suddenly leaned so far forward he was in danger of falling over. "You mean the pretty one? *Wow!* She's amazing! I always thought all girls looked the same, but she's fantastic! What's her name? Hey, maybe I should go and join the party after all!" He pulled himself back onto his feet, his face one big grin.

"No!" the bat squeaked as loudly as he could. *"Keep watching!"*

Marcus hesitated. There was urgency in the bat's squeak, and reluctantly he looked down again. "She's talking to Arry," he said. "Nina-Rose is looking pretty sick. Now she's walking Arry away into the rose garden—hey! Guess what? They're going into the rose bower together. Rats! I can't see them clearly . . . oh. Oh, no." Marcus went pale.

"Tell me, kiddo!"

"It's that purple smoke. . . . I saw it once before."

"That's bad," the bat said grimly. "What's happening now?"

"She's coming out on her own and"—Marcus rubbed his eyes furiously—"she's holding a *frog!* That's so weird! Now she's shoved the frog into her basket, and she's sort of skipping away. . . . What's going on? I don't understand—why isn't Arry coming out?"

"Just keep watching," the bat said.

"The frog girl's heading for the Royal Pavilion. Oh! She's met Prince Albion! He's talking to her and—yuck!—he's kissing her hand. Oh, and there's little Prince Vincent too—"

Marcus's voice was drowned out by a trumpet call,

followed by the Dreghorn Brass Band bursting into a foot-tapping version of the conga. The bat groaned, flapped out of the shade, and landed on Marcus's shoulder. "Keep looking," he urged. "What's the scene?"

"They're all dancing," Marcus reported. "But I still can't see Arry—"

"The girl!" the bat hissed. "What's *she* doing?"

"She's dancing too. She's at the head of a line. . . . there's Vincent and Albion and Tertius too—and Fedora's there, but she doesn't look too keen, she's just hanging on to Tertius—and Nina-Rose as well, and about six of Nina-Rose's little sisters. They're doing the conga in and out of the tents—they look hysterical! Albion looks like a total idiot! Now she's leading them around the Pavilion and across the yard to the walled garden." Marcus snapped his fingers in time with the music. "Di-da-da-da-*dah*-da, di-da-da-da-*dah*-da! Nina-Rose's little sisters have had enough . . . but the rest of them are going around and around and *around* the fountain, and they're laughing like crazy—Hey! They've flung their crowns into the water! What's that frog girl doing? Oh, my sainted *stars*. There's purple smoke everywhere—I can't see. . . . Yes, I can! Oh, no. No! *No!*" Marcus went whiter

than white and clutched at the stone wall for support. *"She's turned them into frogs!"* he whispered. "The fountain's full of them! She's turned them into frogs— *what's she done to Arry?"* Marcus lunged for the tower door.

The bat fluttered wildly in his face. *"Watch her!"* he begged. "See what she does next!"

But it was too late. Marcus was already hurling himself down the ladder. As he reached the belfry, his way was blocked by a burly Dreghornian in national costume.

"Come to see the bells, m'lad?" he inquired cheerfully. "Well, I'd suggest you whiz down them stairs smartish. You don't want to be in 'ere once they starts a-ringing, which they will do any second now."

Marcus seized the man by his suspenders. "Ring them *now!*" he yelled. "There's a witch turning princes into frogs—you've got to warn them! Ring the bells!" And he shot away down the spiral staircase.

The Dreghornian shook his head. "They starts drinking so young these days," he said sadly as he checked his watch. "Exactly three o'clock." He leaned over the stairwell and bellowed, "Let's have those bells, Grebbin!"

The bells rang out as Marcus reached the last step.

At least that'll warn everybody, he thought as he shot out the church door. Seconds later, the sound of cheering swelled up to mingle with the bells. Marcus groaned as he hurtled into the graveyard. "They think it's part of the celebrations! I *have* to get there and tell them. . . . Glee! *Glee!* Where are you?"

But there was no sign of the pony. Marcus groaned again and hurled himself at the thick holly hedge that separated the churchyard from the Royal Gardens. It was a solid hedge, grown to repel the boldest of intruders, but Marcus was desperate. Scratched and bleeding, he emerged at last on the other side to be greeted by a large soldier with his hands on his hips.

"And what do you think you're doing, laddie?" the soldier asked.

Marcus was too breathless to answer at once. He glanced around and saw to his complete astonishment that the celebration party was continuing exactly as before. Crowds of Dreghornians were happily strolling among the tents and stalls, helping themselves from tables groaning under the weight of assorted pies and puddings. Various kings and queens were sitting in the shade of the Royal Pavilion's golden canopy, sipping cooling drinks from silver cups. There was no sign of the frog girl.

"I asked you a question, laddie," the soldier said. "What do you think you're doing? Scruffy little urchin—"

Marcus shut his eyes, yelled, and head-butted the soldier in the stomach as hard as he could. The soldier grunted and collapsed. Marcus seized his opportunity, tore past him, and ran in between the tents until he found his way to the rose garden. Ignoring the shouts behind him, he rushed into the rose arbor . . . and found a small green frog sitting mournfully on a damp patch on the stone floor.

"Ribbit," it said. "Ribbit!"

Chapter Nineteen

By the time Gracie had circled the house for the fourth time, she was getting cross. She was tired, she was hungry, and most of all she was parched with thirst. She stamped her foot sharply, and the path twitched back. "Path!" Gracie said. "Take me to the front door *this minute*! Or . . . or I'll tell the Ancient Crones about you!"

Gracie had no idea if her threat would have any effect, but the path immediately straightened itself and headed toward a small crooked side door covered in ivy.

"*Good* path," Gracie said kindly, and tried not to notice when the path attempted to trip her up at the very last moment. She knocked, and the door opened with a friendly squeak. Cautiously, Gracie stepped inside and looked around. She was standing in a long narrow corridor with at least two dozen doors at the far end. Some were tall and some were tiny, and various messages were tacked or pinned on each.

Gracie hurried to look at the nearest door and was alarmed to read, DO NOT ENTER UNLESS ABLE TO SWIM. The next offered, WATER WINGS: THREE ACORNS AN HOUR. The acorns had been half crossed out, and a scratchy pen had added, PEPPERCORNS PREFERRED, BUT NOT ESSENTIAL.

Gracie moved farther down the corridor and read, HEDGEHOGS ONLY, followed by WEB BUSINESS AND INQUIRIES. "Does that mean inquiries about webs?" She wondered aloud. "Or general inquiries? Oh, dear. I do wish there was someone to ask . . ."

At once a quill pen dripping with violet ink whizzed over her shoulder and attacked the notice fiercely. WEB BUSINESS AND WEB INQUIRIES ONLY! it wrote, and Gracie sighed. The pen spun around and added a tiny PS: IF YOU WANT TEA, TRY DOOR SEVENTEEN. As soon as it had finished, it vanished.

Gracie cheered up at once. She called, "Thank you!" down the empty corridor and began counting doors. "Hmm," she said. "Which end should I begin at?"

The pen reappeared, scratched FOR HEAVEN'S SAKE! on top of HEDGEHOGS ONLY, dropped a large violet blob of ink on Gracie's arm, and disappeared again.

Gracie found the seventeenth door and knocked. A crackly voice called, "Come in!" and she turned the handle, her heart pitter-pattering in her chest.

Whatever Gracie had expected, it wasn't what she saw. The room was enormous, with a low, heavily beamed ceiling. It was very warm but very dark; a roaring fire was the only source of light, and as the flames danced and flickered, long dark shadows leaped up and down the walls. Two huge looms dominated the room, and beside each sat an old, old woman; one was tall and skinny with a wig of wild red curls, and the other short and squat with coal-black hair. The tall one was weaving something so fine as to be almost invisible; spidery silver threads hung in the air, and only the steady *clack! clack!* of the shuttles passing to and fro convinced Gracie that there was anything there at all. On the other loom was a spectacular length of the blackest velvet. In the center, between the looms, was a massive armchair that at first glance looked as if it were covered in fur, but as Gracie's eyes grew accustomed to the gloom, she saw a third, even older woman almost entirely covered in cats. She appeared to be asleep, for the one eye in the center of her forehead was firmly closed, and every so often a long echoing snore floated across the room.

The two weavers froze as they saw Gracie.

The silence seemed endless.

Even the snoring stopped.

There was an ominous rumbling, and a silver thread snapped with a sharp *ping!*

"The loom, sister, the loom!" shrieked the red-haired crone, and as the *clack! clack!* began once more, she waved a skinny arm in the air and let out a long banshee wail. "Ayoooooo . . . Here she comes . . . the one for whom we wait!"

"Ayoooooo . . . Gracie Gillypot . . . the one for whom we wait!" droned the other.

"Waiting for you to release us from our labors!" chanted the first. "You will take your place at the loom, so once more we may go back into the world . . ."

"You will take your place at the loom . . ." echoed the other.

Gracie stared at the two old women, trying to fight a tide of rising panic. What did they mean, *take your place at the loom?* "Excuse me," she faltered, "but I think there must be some mistake . . ."

"No, no, no, no!" the red-haired woman intoned. "We are the Ancient Crones, and our task is to spin the web of power . . ."

"The web of power . . ." echoed the other.

"And we may not leave this place until another comes willingly through the door . . ."

"Willingly through the door . . ."

"To weave the web forever and hereafter . . ."

"Ever and hereafter . . ."

Chapter Twenty

Gracie swallowed hard. She was hearing a horrid little voice in her head. Marlon's voice. "Never been too certain of the state of the old heart. Dodgy deals are my business. . . ."

Had Marlon brought her here to turn her into what was, in fact, a slave? Weaving the web forever and hereafter didn't sound much like a nine-to-five job. And what else had he said? Oh, yes. "Change of employment. New line. *Different boss* . . ." Gracie pulled at her pigtails. He had also said that she should trust him . . . but trust him to do what, exactly?

Gracie sighed and, being a practical sort of girl, decided to deal with her most immediate problem. "I don't suppose I could have a drink, could I?" she asked. "The purple pen told me I could have a cup of tea if I came into room seventeen, and this *is* room seventeen, isn't it? I'm quite happy to make it myself, if you show me where the kettle is. Perhaps you'd all like a cup too?"

The effect of Gracie's suggestion was electrifying. The oldest crone sat bolt upright, opened a brilliant blue eye, and shooed the cats away. "Scat!" she said sharply. "Scat!" She turned to Gracie. "Pull the curtains, child, and let's have a proper look at you. There's a cord beside you. And you, Elsie"—she waved an arm at the red-haired woman—"go out and put the kettle on. And bring some cake. The child's probably hungry as well as thirsty!"

Gracie found the cord and pulled. Black velvet curtains flew back from tall windows all around the room, and sunlight poured in. Blinking hard, she moved forward as the oldest crone beckoned her to her side.

"Come along, come along! I won't hurt you. I'm sorry if you were frightened, but we have to keep up appearances. Couldn't be certain Marlon was right about you, you see—sometimes that bat makes terrible errors of judgment. And who would take us seriously if they knew what we were really like? I'm Edna, by the way. You can call me Auntie. The redhead's Elsie—she wears a wig. Bald as an egg underneath. The other one's Val. She doesn't say much. Been here thirty years, and she's pining for the outside world. Silly, if you ask me, but there you are. She's served her term and more besides. Of course, everyone outside knows us as the Youngest, the Oldest, and the Ancient One. *Much* more impressive than Val, Elsie, and Edna, don't you think?"

Gracie could only nod.

"So, Marlon brought you here," Edna went on. "Do you know why?"

Gracie shook her head. "No, ma'am."

Edna's bright blue eye studied Gracie appraisingly. "Hmm. He's up to something. We asked him to find a replacement for Val, but you're much too young. And besides, you're a Trueheart. Working on the web wouldn't teach you anything. You've had a hard life, have you?"

Gracie nodded again. "I was living with my step-father and my stepsister," she said. "They weren't—they weren't always very nice to me."

"Marlon told us as much," Edna said. "He says your stepsister's a werewoman."

"Foyce?" Gracie's eyes opened wide. "She's a *what*?"

"Didn't you know? Her mother was a werewolf. Good at running, is she?"

"Yes," Gracie said.

"Unusually good sense of smell? Excellent hearing?"

Gracie paused. When she came to think about it, it was true. "Yes," she said.

"There you are, then," Edna said. "Ah, here's Elsie. About time, too. Have your tea and cake, child. Afterward you can have a hot bath. Val's due for a rest, so she'll show you to your room. We'll chat again later."

Gracie took her mug of tea most gratefully. "Thank you *so* much," she said. "Erm. Could I ask you something, er . . . Auntie Edna?"

"Of course," Edna said, "if you're quick. I'm about to go back to sleep."

"Is it true?" Gracie asked. "Do you really have to keep the looms working all the time?"

"The loom that spins the web must never stop. We use the other for orders. Clothes and so on." Edna looked pleased with herself. "We charge a fortune. Keeps us in cake and other necessities."

"What happens if it does stop?" Gracie wanted to know.

Edna frowned. "We don't exactly know," she said slowly. "We daren't risk finding out. There's Magic outside, and it's been there much longer than I've been here. You must have noticed the Unwilling Bushes, and the Bogs of Unimaginable Depths, and the Mires of Sinking Sand . . ."

"I certainly found the bushes," Gracie said with feeling, "but I didn't see any mires or bogs."

"Goodness! You *are* a Trueheart!" Edna said. "Well done! But those things are there to protect the web, so the web *must* be powerful—so we need to keep weaving. If you ask me, I think the web acts as a filter. It helps to keep good and evil in balance. And it's been throwing a dark shadow just the last few days, so there must be something wicked stirring out there that we need to keep an eye on."

Gracie didn't understand. "I think I'll ask you to explain again after my bath," she said, and yawned. "I'm so sorry—but we were walking a very long way. . . ."

"You poor dear," Edna said. "Of course you need a rest. Elsie's back, so Val will show you around. See you later on. . . ."

And as Edna settled herself under her cats, Gracie, yawning fit to burst, followed Val out of door seventeen, along the corridor, and into HEDGEHOGS ONLY. There she found a ramshackle four-poster bed, a tin bath full of steaming hot water, and a heap of fluffy white towels.

"Enjoy!" Val said, and left Gracie to have a gloriously hot bath, followed by a long, dreamless sleep.

Chapter Twenty-one

Foyce was glowing with pride. As she sauntered away from the walled garden, the band broke into a waltz, and she danced a few steps with her basket before making her way back into the heart of the celebrations. She had completed her mission, and so far nobody had noticed. As she floated past the Royal Pavilion, she heard murmurs of "Has anyone seen Prince Tertius?" and "Where could Prince Arry have gotten to?" and "Isn't it time those sweet things were getting ready for the Wild Rejoicings?" but on the whole the older members of the various Royal Families were having much too much of a good time to worry about their offspring.

"*There!* There's that horrid, mean girl!"

Foyce turned. The smallest of Nina-Rose's sisters was pointing at her. When she saw Foyce looking at her, she stuck out her tongue.

"You're nasty!" The next youngest was glaring at Foyce too. "We *saw* you! You turned our sister into a *frog*! We *told* on you, but our mommy said we were just telling stories—but we *weren't*! You're *horrid* and we *hate* you!"

Foyce turned her snake-like eyes on the little girls. "I'll turn *you* into frogs if you aren't quiet!" The girls shrieked, and Foyce moved swiftly away. *Time I left,* she thought.

But leaving quietly was harder than she had anticipated. As she moved through the crowded throng, men and boys of all shapes and sizes kept stepping up and offering to fetch her drinks, carry her basket, or bring her the meatiest pie. When a scruffy boy with leaves in his hair and scratches on his face created a sudden diversion by head-butting a soldier, then screaming, *"Witch! Witch! There's a witch in the gardens!"* she took advantage of the chaos and hurried away as fast as she could go.

Lady Lamorna was waiting on the bench beyond the Royal Gates in a fever of anticipation. When she saw Foyce skimming down the drive toward her, she had to force herself to appear quite indifferent.

Foyce blew kisses at the colonel-in-charge as he

opened the gates for her and strolled across the road. "Easy as pie," she said coolly. "They haven't even noticed—"

From behind the gates came the sound of shouting, followed by a great deal of screaming. The colonel blew his bugle, and his company of soldiers regretfully stopped gazing at Foyce and marched swiftly away.

"Well, maybe they have now." Foyce sniggered. "Shall we go?"

"You have the frogs?" Lady Lamorna asked.

Foyce pulled back a corner of the cloth covering her basket, and a tiny indignant voice said, "Oi! You there! Turn me back *at once!*"

Other voices joined in.

"That's right!"

"We'll have you thrown in the dungeons!"

"This is *shocking!*"

"*Please* let us go. . . ."

"Be quiet!" Foyce snapped. "Or I'll drop all of you in the road and stomp on you!"

The frogs fell silent. The sorceress looked at them doubtfully. "I think you should have left them behind," she said. "They seem very noisy."

Foyce frowned. "I've explained it once already,"

she snapped, "and you agreed. Prince—or princess. *Zap!* Frog. Right?"

Lady Lamorna nodded.

"And then we send their weeping mommies and daddies a letter offering your services to change the little croakers back into royal boys and girlies—for a *large* sum of money."

Lady Lamorna decided to ignore the "we." *"We"* was not part of her plan. She nodded again.

"Well, they'll try anything not to pay that much." Foyce rolled her eyes. "Royalty's like that. Cheap as weasels. They'll try that cheapo magician in Niven's Knowe first, and then the old wizard in Cockenzie Rood, and then the Witches of Wadingburn—and we can't risk them succeeding, can we?"

Lady Lamorna drew herself up to her full height. *"No one* can break my spells except me," she announced.

"But we don't know for certain, do we?" Foyce insisted. "Suppose they got lucky? But now I've swapped the royal croakers for ordinary ditch frogs; there's nothing they can do. They can wave their wands over them until they're blue in the face. We'll keep *these* little beauties safe and sound—and they'll *have* to agree to our terms!" And Foyce smiled proudly.

Naturally, Foyce did not mention her real reason for keeping the frogs in her possession. She was certain Lady Lamorna intended to keep the gold for herself, but she knew that as long as she, Foyce Undershaft, had the royal frogs in her keeping, she could strike a hard bargain.

After a pause Lady Lamorna, whose plans were much as Foyce suspected, said, "Yes. Yes, you may be right."

"I am," Foyce said. "Now, we should be going. It just so happens that I know of the ideal cellar to keep these froggies safe and happy. It's time we went back to Fracture, Your Evilness. Oh, and there's a little bit of business I have to finish in Gorebreath as we pass through. By the way, where's the troll?"

Lady Lamorna glanced around, surprised. "Gubble?" she called.

There was no answer.

Foyce looked at the two donkeys tethered to the back of the bench. "He can't have gone far," she said.

Lady Lamorna, remembering the state Gubble had been in when he and the donkey limped their way back from a stout and unyielding bramble bush on the way to Niven's Knowe, thought the same. Nevertheless, no amount of calling brought any answer. "I had to

teach him a lesson for calling me Evilness in front of the soldiers," she said. "He may be sulking."

Foyce saw an opportunity. "I say we leave the troll."

Having no heart, Lady Lamorna was unable to feel any regret. She did, however, feel it would be inconvenient to do without Gubble.

Seeing her wavering, Foyce said quickly, "When you've got all that gold, you can pay for a hundred servants—servants who'll obey your every word!"

"Indeed." Lady Lamorna swung herself into her saddle with a calculating look in her eye. "How many frogs are there?"

Foyce peered into the basket. "Six."

"Six thousand gold pieces . . . Yes. I will have a hundred servants as well as my robe of skulls." She watched Foyce strapping the basket of frogs firmly onto the back of the second donkey. "Are you not going to ride?"

Foyce shook her head. "I can run," she said. "Let's go. . . ."

Chapter Twenty-two

"Marcus? Is it really you?"

Marcus, swinging from the ham-size fist of a soldier, tried to speak, but his collar was too tight. "Unf," he said.

"Put my son down," his father ordered.

The soldier loosened his grip. "Excuse me, Your Majesty," he said apologetically, "but I found him crawling in through a hedge. And then he was yelling his head off about witches and suchlike, and I couldn't see that he was up to much good—"

The king waved a weary hand. "Please accept my thanks. Marcus, have you heard the terrible news?"

Marcus nodded and sank to one knee. "I know, Father." He fished down the front of his shirt. "Here he is." And he held out a hot and bothered frog.

King Frank stared at him. "Are you mad? This is no time to play stupid games. There's been a kidnapping, my boy—a kidnapping. Arry, Tertius and Fedora, Nina-Rose, Albion of Cockenzie Rood, and little Vincent of Wadingburn—they've all been taken!"

"But they haven't been kidnapped!" Marcus waved the frog under his father's nose. "They're in the fountain! They're—"

"King Frank! King Frank!" Queen Kesta of Dreghorn appeared, puffing hard and clutching a large damp handkerchief. "I came hurrying to tell you, my dear friend. It's so dreadfully utterly *totally* awful! Nina-Rose's sisters saw it happen—but when they told me, of course I didn't believe them for a minute. I mean, imagine! A pretty girl turning our dear ones into frogs! *Such* a story, I thought, and I was quite cross with my little precious pearls. But then they came back a little later looking *so* pale, and I just *knew* there was something wrong because I *do* have a mother's instinct, and they said they'd seen the witch again and she'd said she would turn *them* into frogs too! So their father went with them, just to keep them quiet, you know, and they took him to the fountain, and there they all were—their crowns lying in the water beside them! Oh, imagine it!

My beautiful Nina-Rose a horrible slimy *frog*!" And she collapsed on Marcus's father in a fit of sobbing.

King Frank handed her to the soldier and folded his arms. "We must take action at *once*!" he said. "Whoever has done this dreadful thing must be found and punished!" He stopped and rubbed his head. "No! No, the first thing we must do is restore them to themselves. Call the magicians, the wizards—anybody who can remove this terrible spell! Put up notices! Send messengers throughout the land! Offer a reward—yes! Offer a large reward!" He stooped down to the wilting Queen Kesta. "Don't you agree?"

"Anything!" she wailed. "Anything that will bring my darling back to me!"

"We'll call a council immediately!" King Frank declared. He hauled Queen Kesta to her feet. "We'll hold it in the Royal Pavilion!" He was about to hurry away when he remembered Marcus. "Soldier! Make sure my other son is kept safe! There may be more witchery yet."

"Sir!" The soldier saluted, then turned to look for Marcus . . . but Marcus was long gone. Queen Kesta's arrival had momentarily distracted him, and the frog had taken a leap for freedom. Marcus had dived after it, and as he caught it, an incredibly clear thought flashed into his head. *This isn't Arry! Arry would never run away from me!*

Pushing his way back through the holly hedge, Marcus made his way to a gravestone and sat down to study the frog. It sat nervously on the palm of his hand, panting hard.

"Frog," Marcus said, "are you Arry? Because I don't think you are. If I'm wrong, wave a leg."

The frog didn't move.

"OK. We'll try again," Marcus said patiently. "If you're *not* Arry, wave a leg."

The frog still didn't move.

"Kiddo," a familiar voice said, "it's a *frog*. Plain, ordinary, tribe of tadpole. Let it go."

Marcus wheeled around. The bat was in the shade of the hedge, and Marcus stared at him. "So where's Arry? You seem to know so much about everything. Where *is* he?"

"Think, kiddo . . . think! What did you see when the dame came out of that arbor place?"

Marcus screwed up his eyes to remember. "She was carrying her basket . . . *and I saw her put a frog inside*! Was *that* Arry?"

"You hit the nail right on the head," the bat said. "That dame was catching frogs this morning like it was going out of style. Betcha she did that with all the kids. Swapped 'em. Not what we expected. Clever bit of work, that dame."

Marcus gaped, his mind spinning. "You mean she changed Arry into a frog, then took him and left a *real* frog in his place?"

The bat sighed. "The prof said you were quick on the uptake. Guess even a prof can be wrong."

"The professor?" Marcus did more gaping. "You know the *professor*?"

"Who d'you think put me up to chasing you around, kiddo? I don't do charity." The bat sounded peevish. "You never noticed me checking you out in that bookstack of yours?"

Marcus, trying hard to absorb this new information, gently put the frog on the grass. It hopped away without a backward glance. "Sorry," he said, and stood up. "So we have to find that girl—what did you say her name was?"

"Foyce. And what's with the *we*? This is *your* adventure, kiddo." The bat yawned. "Not to say I don't have an interest, but it's you at ground level. Me—I need a break. All this day stuff—wears a fellow out.

See ya later!" He flipped a wing, soared up toward the church tower, and vanished. A second later he flew a loop over Marcus's head. "Fracture," he called down. "Look for the dame in Fracture. . . ." And he was gone.

"Wait!" Marcus yelled, but the only reply was a snuffle and the clink of a bridle. "Glee," Marcus said as the pony butted him affectionately. "Oh, Glee! Am I glad to see you. . . ." He put his arms around his pony's neck and burst into tears. "Oh, Glee, we've got to find Arry—but I don't know where to go! Where's Fracture?"

"Evilness," grunted a headstone. "Prince. *Zap!* Frog."

Marcus hastily wiped his eyes. "Come on out, troll!" he said as bravely as he could. He pulled the map out of his pocket and rolled it into a tube. "I'm . . . I'm ready for you!"

Chapter Twenty-three

Gracie woke up slowly and lay wondering if she'd died and gone to heaven. Never in her life had she had smooth white sheets, or soft pillows, or a feather bed that rustled comfortingly every time she moved. She turned over luxuriously, enjoying the warmth.

There was a tap on her door, and she sat up. "Hello?" she said, and Val came in carrying a tray laden with boiled eggs, toast dripping with butter, a jar of marmalade, and a mug of hot milk.

"*Wow,*" Gracie breathed. "Thank you *so* much."

"Ancient says she'll see you after," Val said brusquely.

"I'll be as quick as I can." Gracie hesitated. "Excuse me for asking—but do you want to be back in the world very badly?"

Val's eyes filled with tears. "I have a brother I'd like to see," she said. "I hear news of him, but it's not the same. We planned to retire together . . . take a little cottage . . ."

"I'm so sorry," Gracie said. "And you can't leave until someone else comes to take your place?"

Val heaved a heavy sigh. "Who would want to stay here?" she asked.

"Well . . ." Gracie said, "I was thinking. Maybe when I'm older, I could help out. Perhaps I could do a couple of days a week, or something like that?"

For the first time since Gracie had met her, Val smiled. "You're a real Trueheart," she said. "And thank you. But I'm afraid minding the web is a punishment. You have to be a Falseheart—and a bad one at that—before Ancient takes you on." She saw the look on Gracie's face. "Oh, I'm a Trueheart now. Have been for years—paid my dues in full measure." She looked wistful for a moment. "I felt bad about stealing the treasure chest, but there was *such* a lovely train set inside. It took me years to repent, but I did in the end. I'd better get back. The web's acting up, and Elsie's not as good at handling it as me."

Gracie ate her eggs and toast slowly after Val had gone, enjoying every mouthful. When she got out of bed, she found that her clothes had been washed and ironed, and the rips in her dress had been neatly darned.

They're so kind, she said to herself. *Maybe having a mother would be a bit like this. I wonder what I can do to thank them.* She made her bed neatly, piled her breakfast things on the tray, and carried it out of HEDGEHOGS ONLY.

"There must be a kitchen somewhere," she said hopefully, and the quill pen zoomed over her shoulder and fluttered in front of WATER WINGS.

HOT AND COLD WATER, it wrote at enormous speed. GOOD SLEEP HOPE SO TAKE CARE DANGER. It quivered for a second, then did its usual vanishing trick.

"Thanks!" Gracie called, and opened WATER WINGS's door to find a large and well-equipped kitchen piled high with dirty dishes. *Well, that's something I can help with,* she thought cheerfully as she put down her tray. She filled the sink with scalding water, put as many plates in to soak as would fit, then dried her hands and went to find door seventeen.

The Ancient One was asleep under her cats, but as Gracie coughed politely, she sat bolt upright. "Ah! There you are, my dear. Sleep well?"

"Yes, thank you," Gracie said. She had been about to offer her services in the kitchen, but she was distracted by the web. A dark stain was spreading over the silver fabric, and Elsie was throwing the shuttle to and fro considerably faster than she had been when Gracie saw her last. Val was poring over the fabric with an anxious gaze.

"Things aren't good," Edna said, "and we need your help, if you are willing to give it."

Gracie nodded. "I'd be pleased to," she said. "I was going to offer to wash dishes, but if there's anything else, I'll do that instead. Or as well," she added quickly, in case it sounded as if she was being choosy about doing dishes.

Edna chuckled. "I knew you were just what we needed the moment you offered to make us tea. Now, let me tell you what's happened. While you were asleep, we've had more news." She paused. "Perhaps I should go back to the beginning. Did you know your stepsister followed you?"

"Oh, yes," Gracie said. "Marlon was so clever! We gave her the slip!"

"But she was meant to follow you," Edna said. "That was Marlon's plan—but it went wrong."

Gracie took a sharp breath. "He *meant* her to?

But . . . but he gave me the Trueheart Stew, and she went to sleep! He helped me escape!"

"He never meant Foyce to catch you," Edna reassured her. "He wanted her to follow your trail all the way here so she would be caught by the Unwilling Bushes and the Bogs of Unimaginable Depths. They'd have held her fast, you see, and we could have bargained with her. Her life in exchange for a shortish spell on the web. A mere fifty years or so would have cured her nicely."

"Erm . . . she's not very easy to bargain with," Gracie said.

A fierce blue fire shone in the Ancient One's eye. "We have our ways" was all she said, but Gracie was suddenly very glad the Ancient One was her friend and not her enemy.

"So what went wrong?" she asked.

Edna leaned forward. "Marlon made a mistake. He forgot that Foyce's mother was a werewolf. A human would have slept for hours, but she was after you in no time at all . . . and as you know, she can run like the wind. He couldn't risk her catching you, so he abandoned his plan and brought you here as fast as possible." Edna's one blue eye twinkled. "For once he was a bat of his word. It seems you are his hero,

Gracie Gillypot. He thinks you can hear spiders laugh."

Gracie looked guilty. "And I thought he'd abandoned me . . . but what do you want me to do?"

The Ancient One stopped twinkling and looked serious. "Is your True Heart also a brave one?"

"Um." Gracie thought about it. "I don't think I know. But I can try to be brave."

"A good answer. Now, Foyce has joined forces with Lady Lamorna of Fracture Castle. We knew the old sorceress had a plan—a very simple plan. She intended to turn a number of princes into frogs, then demand gold in return for restoring them to human form. She needs, you see, to pay for a new dress." For a fraction of a second, the Ancient One of the House of Crones looked extremely smug. "A very beautiful new dress. Embroidered with spiders, and—"

Elsie cleared her throat in a meaningful way, and Edna lost the dreamy look in her eye.

"So," she went on briskly, "we've been standing by, waiting for messengers from the palaces to come riding up to ask for help. We have antidotes, you see. In the words of Lady Lamorna's servant, 'Frog. *Zap!* Prince.' Unfortunately, Foyce has tangled this plan and now has the six royal frogs in her power—and Foyce has ambitions far beyond those of the aged Lady Lamorna."

"So what do you want me to do?" Gracie asked.

The Ancient One looked straight at her. "We want you to go to Fracture and find the frogs. We want you to bring them here so we can remove the enchantment. We want Foyce to follow you, because it is essential for the kingdoms of the Northern Plains that she is kept under our watching eye. There will be help—Marlon has sent word that a young prince, Marcus, will meet you on your way. His brother is among the royal frogs."

"Oh." Gracie looked down at her bare feet so Edna couldn't see how scared she felt. When she looked up, she was grinning. "Shall I wash the dishes before I go or after I get back?"

There was a tiny flutter of applause, and Gracie saw a bat balanced on the top of the curtains.

"Marlon!" she said. "I'm *so* pleased—"

"Tch!" Edna interrupted her. "That's *Millie*, dear." She dropped her voice to a whisper. "You mustn't make the mistake of thinking they all look alike." Then, in her normal tone, she went on: "Marlon is recovering from heat exhaustion in Dreghorn church tower, so Millie has offered to be your guide. By the way, she's Marlon's daughter."

Gracie was surprised. Somehow she had never thought of Marlon as a family bat. She waved at Millie. "How do you do? It's very kind of you to help me."

Millie flew down from the curtains and looped the loop. "Delighted, I'm sure," she said. "Are you ready?"

"I'm ready," Gracie said.

Chapter Twenty-four

Lady Lamorna hardly spoke on the long journey back to Fracture. The realization that Foyce had out-maneuvered her grew clearer with every step, but she could see no way of regaining her power over the girl. Foyce had the royal frogs and was obviously deter-mined to keep them in her possession until she was paid, and paid handsomely at that.

Although Lady Lamorna still had spell powder in her traveling bag, she was uneasily aware that there was very little left. Only a few pinches. And would the frog spell work on the daughter of a werewolf, or might something much, much worse result? The old sorceress was not given to berating herself, but she could not help but think she had made a mistake. Possibly the worst of her whole life.

The road seemed endless. Foyce had insisted they stop briefly in Gorebreath while she sniffed her way up and down the two main streets. She said she was looking for a sister, but to Lady Lamorna she had the air of a ferret hunting down a featherless chick. No sister was found, and Foyce took out her frustration on the donkey burdened with the royal frogs. She slapped him so hard he took off at a gallop, and although Foyce easily kept pace with him, Lady Lamorna was hard pressed to keep her in sight.

What if she gets away from me? the sorceress worried. *What can I do?* Even the knowledge that she alone could restore the frogs to their human form was of little comfort. She found herself longing for the familiar shambling shape of Gubble. Gubble, who was devoted to her. Gubble, whom she could have ordered to bite, bite, *bite* . . .

Chapter Twenty-five

If Lady Lamorna could have seen Gubble at that very moment, she might have given way to complete despair. Gubble was, for Gubble, looking cheerful. He was not a long way behind the sorceress and Foyce, and he was riding Marcus's pony with a fair degree of success. There was something like a grin spread over his flat green face, and every so often a deep rumble shook him from head to foot. Marcus, alarmed at first, had decided that this was Gubble's way of laughing and grinned back.

When the bedraggled figure had first limped out from behind the gravestone, Marcus had reeled away in horror. But Glee had pushed him forward to look again.

"Help Gubble," the troll said hopefully. "Gubble help boy."

Marcus stared. "Did you know your head is on back to front?" was all he could think to say.

"Gubble knows." A tear dribbled a green channel down Gubble's muddy face.

Marcus studied Gubble carefully. "Don't you work for that witch?" he asked. "I saw you with her!"

The troll's face screwed itself into an expression of intense hatred. "No more Evilness," he spat. "Gubble's Trouble, Evilness is."

Marcus was impressed. "What about that girl— Foyce?" he said.

Gubble's face grew even more livid. "Gubble hate girl."

"But I've got to find her," Marcus explained. "She's got my brother! I have to rescue him—him and the others. Can you show me the quickest way to Fracture? I've got a map, but I'd be quicker with a guide. . . ."

Gubble tried to nod, but his shoulders got in the way. "Gubble knows," he said. Then again, "Help Gubble!"

"I'll do my best," Marcus said. "I'll have to get the spell taken off Arry somehow—so whoever does that could help you too. If someone can take the spell off a frog, it should be easy for them to swap your head around." He put his foot in his stirrup, then paused. "Would you like to ride Glee? I'll run for a bit. Erm . . . which way do you want to face?"

After a short experiment, it appeared that Gubble felt happiest with his body facing backward, his head looking forward. This meant that he could hold firmly on to the back of Glee's saddle, and he felt safer than he ever had riding on the donkey. "Nice!" he said approvingly.

"Let's go," Marcus said, and they left the church-yard to cut across the fields, Glee trotting steadily and Marcus running alongside.

Chapter Twenty-six

As the evening drew on, the clouds sank low and a steady drizzle made the various travelers shiver and pull their cloaks and coats tight around them. Gracie was more than grateful for the thick cloak Val had given her. Marcus wondered how Ger had managed with such a thin jacket and resolved that if he found Arry and was able to get him home safe and sound, the first thing he would do would be to buy Ger a brand-new coat that kept the rain out. Lady Lamorna, huddled in her old peasant woman's woven wool, felt dampness seeping into her bones. Foyce, warm and dry in her fur-lined cape, lessened her pace a little as the narrow path turned muddy and slippery. Only Gubble was happy. His rumblings became a steady drone, and Marcus suspected that he was singing.

* * *

In the church tower at Dreghorn, the clock solemnly chimed midnight. There was a small rustling, and Marlon shook himself awake. "Time for a checkup," he told himself, and flew to the window. There he let out a series of high-pitched squeaks, stopped, and listened. From Gorebreath came a clear answer, and then, after a pause, a series of relayed messages came flooding in from far and wide.

"Hmm," he said to himself proudly. "My Millie's a good girl. She's doing well. At the rate she's traveling, she and kiddo numero uno'll be in plenty of time for the action. Kiddo number two's doing good too." He scratched his stomach in a thoughtful way. "We may get that dame yet . . . but it's still early." He yawned a sharp-toothed yawn and flew back to his beam. "Quick doze. Need to keep fresh. Don't want any more mistakes. . . ." And Marlon slept again.

He was woken by the faint light of early morning and the flip-flap of the belfry's resident bats making their way back to bed. After giving his fur a cursory brush, he went back to the window and squeaked again. This time there were fewer replies, but Marlon's eyes lit up. "Thought the rain would slow 'em down," he said, "but they've done well! All of them getting close.

Time to make a move. Better see that the kids are OK. *Ciao,* all!" And he left the local bats to heave a sigh of relief as they got ready for bed. Having Marlon as a lodger meant far too many interruptions.

As he flitted his zigzag way over Gorebreath and up Fracture Mountain toward the village, Marlon was pleased to see that the rain had stopped. There were many footprints and hoofprints in the mud of the narrow highway, he noticed. As he soared higher, he saw Marcus and Gubble wearily picking their way up a half-hidden path that led over steep rocks but cut out many of the bends of the usual road. Glee was tethered below on a small patch of grass.

Marlon swooped down. "Hello, there," he said cheerfully. "Does the troll know he's got his head on back to front?"

Gubble stopped his singing and grunted.

"Hello," Marcus said. "And yes, he does. What do you want?"

Marlon was hurt. "Is that the way to talk to a pal?"

"You said it was *my* adventure." Marcus was grumpy from lack of sleep and soaking-wet boots. "It's fine for you, flitting about. We have to climb."

"See my heart?" Marlon said. "It's bleeding. Thought you'd like to know that the dame's back in her den. But I know when I'm not wanted . . ." He shook his head and flew slowly upward.

"Oops—I'm sorry," Marcus said with real sincerity. "I really am." He lowered his voice. "Is it far now?"

"Well, I never was one to hold a grudge," Marlon said cheerfully, "so I'll check it out." He winked at Gubble and disappeared. Two minutes later, he was back. "Hey! Kiddo! Reinforcements! Follow me—" And he shot off at an angle up the steepest aspect of the slope.

What does he mean, reinforcements? Marcus wondered, but he scrambled after the bat as fast as he could, Gubble struggling behind him.

Chapter Twenty-seven

Gracie had found the journey back to Fracture easier than her journey out, despite the rain. Millie was a chatty little bat, and much concerned for Gracie's comfort, so she took care to pick out the easiest paths. She was very proud of her father and spent much of the journey telling Gracie how busy he was, flying to and fro for the Ancient Crones ("He takes nearly *all* their orders, Miss Gracie!") as well as keeping the bat brethren organized, passing messages from one to the other.

"If you want to find out anything, Miss Gracie, just ask my dad! D'you know he even spends time in the palace library? My mom and me, we say he ought to be a Royal Appointed Bat! He looks at so many books, you wouldn't believe! Whenever the princes leave them open, my dad's in there having a peek just as soon as it's dark. And there's this professor, see—he's Miss Val's brother—and it's ever so sad because she wants to not be an Ancient Crone anymore, but even my dad can't find anyone to take her place."

Millie paused for breath, and Gracie saw the lights of Fracture village twinkling high above them. A deathly cold feeling seeped into her stomach, and she was particularly glad to have the little bat chatting happily in her ear as she climbed.

"But you, Miss, I'm sure you'll be able to do as Auntie Edna says, Miss. If you can lead that nasty stepsister of yours into the mires, you'll be doing us all *such* a favor! 'Cause Miss Val says that when she retires, she'll let me and my mom and my dad all live with her and her brother, see, and we'll be as happy as clams, because my dad's getting on a bit, and it'll do him a world of good to rest—"

"What's that? Who says? Hi, kiddo—having your ear bent by my littl'un, are you?"

Gracie stopped for breath and beamed at Marlon. "We've been having the nicest chat," she said.

"Little old blatherer, she is," Marlon said fondly, and he and Millie rubbed noses as they landed side by side on a twig. The cold feeling in Gracie's stomach was suddenly shot through with a sharper pain. She ignored it resolutely and went on smiling. "Are you here to show me the way back again? I have to rescue some frogs, and Foyce"—Gracie hoped her voice wasn't wobbling—"has to follow me."

"Right on, kiddo. There's a lad and a troll right here on the same mission—wait, and I'll bring them on up." And Marlon was off once again.

"Ooooh!" Millie fluttered her wings and smoothed her fur. "That'll be the prince! Aren't you excited, Miss Gracie? You've never met a prince before, I'll bet—me neither!"

Gracie did remember the Ancient One promising she would have help, but the fact that the boy concerned was a real prince hadn't sunk into her consciousness. She had been studiously avoiding thinking about what she was going to have to do once she got to Fracture, and this included anybody who might be involved—Foyce especially, but all others too. A vague idea of crowns and glitter and velvet floated into her head while Millie twittered and made sure her wings were neat. *I hope he won't want a lot of curtsying,* Gracie thought. *Maybe he'll be very posh and grand.*

But when Marcus hauled himself up from the steep slope below the path, his face red and sweaty with the effort, Gracie saw that he was neither posh nor grand. He was wet, grubby, and tired, but he grinned cheerfully before he leaned back to help the most extraordinary creature that Gracie had ever seen.

Gubble had not traveled well. Even when his head faced the right way around, he was not built for speed and agility. Back to front, his progress was painfully slow, and only grim determination had kept him going—grim determination and two important words that rattled around in his small and confused brain. One word was *Help*, the other *Revenge*. He rolled himself onto the path, and then with Marcus heaving on one arm and Gracie on the other, he finally stood up. "Dead," he announced. "Gubble dead."

Marcus slapped him on the front. "Not yet," he said encouragingly. "Remember? We're going to get your head sorted out for you."

Gubble didn't answer. He was squinching up his eyes and staring at the lights on the hill above. "Evilness," he said. "Girl." And his face screwed up into an expression of extreme loathing.

"That's right," Marcus said. He turned to Gracie. "Hi, I'm Marcus. And this," he added, patting Gubble again, "is Gubble."

"OK, OK, OK—no time for chitchat!" Marlon

whizzed in between and around the figures standing on the path. "Got to plan!"

"Actually," Marcus said as he leaned heavily against a mossy tree trunk, "I need a rest. Just for a moment," he added hastily.

"Looks completely wiped out, doesn't he, Miss?" Millie said in Gracie's ear. "Poor lad! Should have stopped for forty winks like we did."

Gracie thought Millie was right. Marcus was now very pale and plastered with mud.

Marlon did another circuit. "No time for that now, kiddo!" he said bossily. "Got to have some action!"

"If we go farther up the hill," Gracie said, "there's an empty house. It's the nearest house to ours—I mean, to Foyce and my stepdad. We could creep in there while it's still dark, and we could plan what to do and rest." Before Marlon could interrupt, she added firmly, "It won't help anyone if we're all worn out."

"Sounds good to me." Marcus managed an exhausted smile.

"Very well said, Miss," Millie said approvingly.

An idea came to Gracie as the little bat fluttered on her shoulder. "Millie," she said, "would you and your dad be able to check something? I'm sure Foyce will

put the frogs in the cellar . . . but we need to know for sure. And is she in the house?"

"Wilco!" Marlon answered for himself and his daughter. "Better check the old one as well. Lady L." He saw Gracie looking puzzled and explained. "Lady Lamorna. Sorceress from the castle — she had the spells, kiddo."

"Oh, *yes*." Gracie nodded. "I'm so sorry. I'd forgotten. I must be tired too."

"Let's get to that house," Marcus said.

Chapter Twenty-eight

Marcus lay down on a pile of rags and fell right asleep. Gubble found an old cupboard, tucked himself inside, and snored.

Gracie stayed wide awake. Her heart refused to settle in her chest, and she was acutely aware of the shabby old house just a little farther up the hill that had been her home for so long. Where was Foyce? And what about Mange? The wind rattled at the broken-down door behind her, and she jumped. She got up quietly and went to look, but there was nothing and no one stirring. Another thought seized her. What if Foyce could smell them? What if the smell of the travelers was, even now, floating up on the wind? Gracie licked her finger and held up her hand. No. Fortune was on their side.

"Hello there, kiddo!" It was Marlon, with Millie close behind, her eyes shining.

"Oh, Miss, you'll never guess! There's an old man asleep on the table in the kitchen, and that girl booted him *ever* so hard and he didn't even stir! Dad says he's never, ever known Trueheart Stew to work so well, and he must be a real bad 'un to sleep so long!"

"Shut it, babe," Marlon told her, not unkindly. "That's the kiddo's stepdad."

Millie began to twitter in embarrassment, but Gracie stopped her. "He's not good at all," she said. "Did you find the frogs? Is Foyce there?"

Marlon nodded. "Frogs are locked in the cellar," he reported. "Hopping about and complaining." He chuckled. "One of them keeps threatening to have everyone's head chopped off."

"Oh, dear," Gracie said. "And Foyce?"

"Writing," Marlon said.

Gracie looked astonished. *"Writing?"*

"Looked over her shoulder. Busy writing letters to the kings. And queens." He snorted, then laughed. "Double-crossing Lady L, if you ask me—Lady L's up there in her castle writing too. *And* she can spell better. A bit."

Millie giggled. "Dad says they can't neither of them

spell *blackmail*. *He* can. My dad was taught by the professor at the castle, my dad was—"

"That's enough, now, Mill. Thought of a plan yet, kiddo?"

Gracie looked thoughtful. "I've had an idea. . . ." she said slowly. "The real problem is getting the frogs out of the cellar. I think we'll have to wait until Foyce goes to bed. I know where she keeps the key. . . . And then once we've got the frogs, we'll have to run for the House of the Ancient Crones and hope for the best."

"I've got a suggestion," Marlon said.

"Yes?" Gracie looked at him hopefully.

"You'll get caught if you run. 'Scuse me, but that dame goes fast. *Real* fast. But the kid's pony, that's faster."

"Hey!" It was Marcus, sitting up and looking considerably brighter. "That's a brilliant idea! You mean, if one of us takes the frogs and rides Glee—"

Marlon shook his head. "Sorry, kiddo. Send the frogs, but no rider. Pony'll be twice as fast."

"That's true," Marcus admitted. "But how will he know where to go?"

Marlon put his wing proudly around Millie. "My girl here—she'll sit in his ear. Knows the way backward, she does, night or day. Your job"—he looked at Gracie and Marcus—"is to keep the dame from catching you. And I'll stick with you."

"That sounds fine," Gracie said. "But what about the troll—Gubble? He can't go very fast. . . ."

A voice from the cupboard growled, "Bite. Gubble bite. Gubble stay and bite."

Marlon, Gracie, and Marcus looked at each other. If Gubble was able to hold Foyce back . . . even for a little while . . .

"Then send help for Gubble," the voice said.

Marcus leaped up and flung open the cupboard door. "I promise," he said. "Gubble, you have the word of Prince Marcus of Gorebreath."

"Gubble not need word. Gubble need *help,*" Gubble said, but he stumbled out and grabbed at Marcus's hand. There were fresh tear tracks on his face, and Gracie fished in her pocket for a hankie.

"Bother," she said as she pulled out the scrap of material. "I keep forgetting I've only got the Trueheart Stew wrapping."

"Babe!" Marlon fell off the curtain rod in his excitement and made a double loop to avoid crashing to the floor. "You still got that? Keep it safe—guard it with your *life!*"

Gracie put the scrap back in her pocket. "Why?"

"When we get to the stream," Marlon said, "*drop it in*! It might just work. But now"—he stretched out his leathery wings—"I'm off to check on the dame. Be back as soon as she's snoring. *Ciao!*"

Chapter Twenty-nine

Even Gracie dozed a little while Marlon kept watch on Foyce and the ever-sleeping Mange. Before it was full daylight, Marcus crept out to fetch Glee and to rub him down with a handful of straw. The pony was fresh and eager to be moving, and Marcus whispered soothingly in his ear while he was grooming him. "You've got to run like the wind when the time comes," he told him. "Go like you never have before." The pony rubbed his head lovingly on Marcus's arm, and Marcus was sure he'd understood. Then Millie came whizzing in to join them, and Marcus solemnly introduced Glee to Millie and Millie to Glee. Millie, overcome by the thought of being in charge of a pony belonging to a real prince, was surprisingly quiet, but Marcus was pleased to see that she and Glee seemed comfortable with each other. He gave Glee a final pat and was creeping back to the empty house when Marlon appeared.

"Flat out and snoring," the bat announced.

"Great," Marcus said. "I'll wake Gracie and Gubble."

Years of experience had taught Gracie how to open the back door of her old home without making a sound, and she, Gubble, and Marcus tiptoed over the threshold and into the kitchen. Mange lay exactly as Gracie had seen him last, crashed out on the kitchen table, and Foyce was sprawled over a heap of paper. A battered pen dripped ink onto the floor. Seeing it reminded Gracie of the purple quill in the House of the Ancient Crones, and she wondered if she would ever be there again. Pushing the thought to one side, she moved silently to the line of bent hooks over the stove.

The cellar key was gone.

Gracie bit her lip and turned to look at the sleeping Foyce. The key must be in her pocket. Grimly, Gracie crept toward her stepsister. She knew that every wolfish sense Foyce possessed would be alerted if she was touched, but it had to be tried. A movement caught her eye, and she saw Marcus pointing furiously to the cellar door.

The key was in the lock! Gracie almost laughed. It was a matter of seconds to get the door open and to slip through and down the steep stone steps. There was very little light, and her eyes seemed to be taking forever to get used to the gloom. She put her hand out into the darkness and felt a cold, clammy frog.

"Excuse *me*, young woman," said a sharp little voice, "but—"

"Shh!" Gracie put her finger to her lips. "*Please* be quiet! I've come to rescue you—can you come over here?" There was the sound of flippered feet, and Gracie was surrounded. She could just make out the shape of the basket flung on the ground, and she pulled it gently toward her. "Could you be very kind and hop in?" she whispered. "You're going to the Ancient Crones. They'll take the spell off, I promise—but you'll have to be patient. There's a bit of a ride first—"

Five frogs hopped into the basket, but the sixth stood back. "And why should we trust you?" he asked coldly.

There was a sharp whisper from the top of the stairs. "Albion? Don't be such a brat. It's me, Marcus from Gorebreath. Get into that basket, or I'll tell everyone where you got that fish you said you caught—"

"OK, OK. A fella's got to be careful, though." The frog glared at Gracie and settled himself in the basket.

Gracie picked the basket up and climbed carefully out of the cellar. As she passed Foyce, her stepsister snorted and moved in her sleep. Gracie's heart began to race as she handed the basket to Marcus. "Quick!" she mouthed.

Marcus nodded. He hurried outside to where Millie and Glee were waiting. "Everything's fine, Arry," he whispered just before he tied on the lid. "See you soon, bro'. . . ." He swung the basket onto Glee's saddle and strapped it on tight. "Good luck—and go, boy, *go*!"

Glee needed no second invitation. He had been pacing up and down, wishing for nothing more than to escape the strange feelings that were floating in the air around him. With Millie safely in place, he neighed a loud and derisive farewell and set off at a gallop.

Foyce sat up. "So the little worm's come back, has she?" she sneered. "Right!" Her voice grew louder. "I've got a score to settle with you!"

Chapter Thirty

Gracie froze, caught in the stare of Foyce's snake eyes. Outside the open door Marcus groaned and pulled the battered map from his pocket. It was the only thing he had that was anything like a weapon, and he rolled it as tightly as he could. It felt curiously heavy in his hand, and he swung it as he headed for the kitchen.

Inside, Foyce was moving stealthily toward Gracie, her eyes gleaming. Gracie backed away, but Foyce was between her and the door. "Slug," she hissed. "Worm. Toad—" A sudden suspicion made her glance away from her stepsister to the cellar door. Seeing it open, she let out a howl of rage and sprang at Gracie, clawing at her face—but she couldn't reach her.

"Bite," said Gubble in muffled tones, his mouth full of dress and ankle. "Gubble stay—"

Marcus leaped across the doorstep and grabbed Gracie's hand. "Run!" he yelled. "Hang on to her, Gubble—do your best—" And he and Gracie pelted out as fast as they could go, straight into the warm fur and rock-solid body of a donkey. Lady Lamorna, caught completely unawares, fell forward on the donkey's neck, and the contents of the leather purse in her hand flew up in the air. Purple dust swirled in all directions, and Marcus threw himself on top of Gracie to protect her. As a last thought he pulled the map as far over his head as he was able.

Shrieks and thumps came loudly from the kitchen, but outside there was complete silence.

Marcus cautiously moved the map. He seemed to be alive, and still a boy. He looked at Gracie. She was sitting up, her face pale, but definitely still a girl.

"That was one lucky escape, kiddo." Marlon appeared above them. "Whatever's in that map? But best get moving—"

Marcus staggered to his feet, pulling Gracie after him. It wasn't easy, because they were directly under the feet of a statue, the stone statue of a donkey and an ancient woman. The woman's stone face was contorted with anger and surprise, but it was still possible to see evil in her eyes. In fact, as Marcus moved

away, the eyes watched him, alive and glittering in the unmoving stone. "Phew," Marcus said. He looked at the map wonderingly. "The professor said I should look after it—"

"*KIDDO!*" Marlon's voice was urgent. "The dame's winning! Scat!"

And Marcus and Gracie scatted. They ran and they ran, Marlon always flittering in front of them, showing them which way to go. They tore through bushes and scrambled up and down hills, and as they ran, Marlon encouraged them.

Every so often he would fly high to check if they were being followed, and the sun was high and hot when he dropped down to hiss, "I can see her. Boy is she mad! But she's limping now. Hurry—the stream's not far. . . ."

They forced themselves on. When the small stream crossed their path, Marlon yelled, "Now!" and Gracie dropped the tiny scrap of Trueheart cloth into the muddy water.

There was no reaction.

"Sorry, kids. Keep running," Marlon urged. Marcus and Gracie didn't need telling, and they struggled on and on, even though Gracie had a stitch that was tearing her in two and Marcus's breath was rasping in his throat.

From behind them came an ear-piercing shriek. Marlon soared into the air and came back, grinning for the first time since they had left.

"You did it, kid," he said. "She can't cross—she'll have to go around by the bridge. That'll hold her up awhile. We might do it yet!"

Chapter Thirty-one

As Foyce, her eyes red and smarting from the Trueheart mists that floated above the stream, raged her way back to find the bridge, her father finally woke from his Trueheart sleep. He yawned, and stretched, and stared in astonishment at the chaos in the kitchen. His chair and the table were the only items that remained as he remembered; everything else was upside down or smashed into a thousand pieces. "Gracie!" he yelled. "Foyce!"

There was no answer.

Mange heaved himself onto his feet and staggered across the room. He peered into the darkness of the cellar, but there was no sign of anyone down there. He stumbled up the ramshackle stairs to the two small bedrooms. Nobody there either, but as he moved past

the window of the smaller bedroom, something outside caught his eye, and he stopped to look.

A statue?

Since when had there been a statue of a ragged
woman on a donkey outside his house?

Mange shook his head and looked again. Now he
saw he had been mistaken. It wasn't a statue after all.
The woman was moving, albeit very slowly. She was
frowning, and muttering, and peering into some kind
of leather pouch.

Mange's heavy eyes brightened. The woman was
old, and she was slow, and she was holding a purse. A
large purse. This was a combination he liked. He
turned and headed for the stairs.

Lady Lamorna climbed stiffly off the donkey, noticing
as she did so that its eyes were frozen open in a look
of complete astonishment. The spell was evidently still
affecting it, but even as she looked she saw an ear
twitch.

"At least I'll be able to get back to my castle,"
she told herself wearily. "But what then? That girl's long
gone. I heard her screeching. Oh, if only I'd turned her
to stone . . . If only I'd never seen her . . . If only I'd
never had anything to do with the world outside . . ."

Lady Lamorna was stopped in her regrets by the sound of a door opening. A man stepped out of the house, blinking in the bright sunlight. There was something about his shambling gait that reminded her of something. Something familiar. Something familiar, and *useful* . . .

An idea edged itself into her mind. One glance at his close-set eyes and thin acquisitive nose assured her that he was both mean and ruthless, qualities that were high on Lady Lamorna's list of essential requirements. He was smiling at her now—at least, she assumed that was what he intended, even though it had more the appearance of a black-toothed leer— and moving toward her. She furtively peeked into her leather pouch.

A pinch of spell powder was all that remained. One pinch only.

It will be enough, Lady Lamorna thought. *It's a long time since I had a human to train. . . . Was Gubble once a human? I don't remember. It will kill the hours while I think of other ways to pay for my dress. Oh, that dress . . . that beautiful dress!*

She took the pinch of spell powder in her skeletal fingers and lifted it high—just as Mange lunged for the purse.

"Be *mine!*" hissed Lady Lamorna, and sprinkled the powder in the air.

Mange froze for a second, then swore. He swore with eloquence and real venom, and Lady Lamorna smiled more cheerfully than she had for a long time.

"What an ideal servant you will make," she remarked. "Now the donkey has shaken free of its spell at last. Let us go."

"I'm not going anywhere," Mange growled. "Give me my foot back!"

"Certainly not," his new mistress said. "Your foot will remain a lump of stone until you have served me for at least fifty years. Or, of course, until I'm tired of you."

Mange gulped. His foot was indeed a lump of stone, and although he could move, it was only with much effort. He was also becoming increasingly aware of a huge power emanating from the old woman that he was totally unable to ignore. Desperately he tried to think of a way to escape his fate. "I'll give you . . . I'll give you gold," he said at last.

"Gold?" If Lady Lamorna had had a heart, it would have leaped. As it was, she stared at Mange, her silver eyes gleaming. "How much gold?"

"Wait!" Mange, dragging his stone foot behind him, half ran, half hobbled into the house. He came back clutching a wooden, brass-bound box and thrust it into Lady Lamorna's arms. "Now let me go," he whined. "Give me my foot back. . . ."

Lady Lamorna opened the box very slowly.

Was it possible? Could it really be that, after all her terrible experiences, she was now to be rewarded for her efforts?

As she saw the shining gold she had to bite back a sigh of relief. The dress was hers.

And so was her new servant.

"I will take your gold," she said graciously. "Perhaps now I will consider letting you go after thirty years—or, then again, perhaps not." She climbed back on her donkey, the box under her arm. "Come! We will celebrate our new arrangement with cakes and wine!" She did not think it worth mentioning that it would be she who did the celebrating, while Mange fetched and carried.

And Mange Undershaft was unable to refuse. Despite all attempts to stay exactly where he was, his body took not the slightest notice of his wishes. He found himself following the sorceress obediently as she rode slowly away.

Chapter Thirty-two

As the sun rolled on around the sky, Gracie and Marcus ran. And ran. The shadows were lengthening when Marlon reported that Foyce was once again in sight. He landed on Marcus's shoulder, and Gracie saw that he was exhausted. His eyes were dull and his fur was matted, and he was panting hard.

"Been a long day," Marlon apologized when he saw her looking. "And sunshine. Doesn't do the eyes no good."

"Is she coming fast?" Gracie asked.

Marlon didn't answer. He was clinging to Marcus's jacket and already asleep.

"Do you know the way, Gracie?" Marcus gasped.

"Tell you when we get to the top of that hill." Gracie stopped to double up and ease her stitch. As she straightened, she felt the beat of running feet in the ground beneath her. "Oh, no . . ." she said. "Oh, *no*—come *on!*"

Panic gave them wings, and they tore up the hill as if their weariness had fallen away.

At the top Gracie let out a long sigh of relief. "Look!" she said. "Can you see? Down there—under the green smoke?"

"Wow! Weird or what?" Marcus said. "And what's that path doing?"

"You'll see," Gracie told him. "Oh, she's nearer! I can hear her now! Run!"

"Could we hide?" Marcus was close beside her as they tumbled and fell into a clump of brambles.

"She'll smell us out," Gracie wailed. "Listen—she's *really* close—she's going to catch us."

Marcus stopped. "You go on," he said. "I'll hold her back for as long as I can. It's the frogs she wants. The frogs and you—not me." He gave Gracie a parting push, stepped out from the bush—and *"GUBBLE!"* he yelled. "Gubble! Gracie, look who it is! It's *Gubble!*"

Gubble was somewhere around two hundred years old, but never in all that time had anyone greeted him with such enthusiasm. He positively beamed as he slid off the donkey.

"Your head's the right way around!" Marcus said. "What happened?"

"Head fell off," Gubble explained. "Head bite girl, girl kick. Gubble more careful. Head back this way."

"Where did you get the donkey from?" Gracie asked.

"It must have been following Lady Lamorna," Marcus guessed. "But Gubble—how did you stay on so well?"

Gubble turned a curious purple, and Gracie guessed he was blushing.

"I know!" she said. "You rode back to front!"

"We'd better keep going," Marcus said. "Gubble, did you see Foyce? Is she far away?"

Gubble looked blank.

"You'd better get back on the donkey," Gracie said. "I know we're nearly there, but she might still catch us."

Between them, Marcus and Gracie helped Gubble back onto the donkey, which set off again at a fast trot. It seemed to know exactly where it was going, and at first Marcus and Gracie ran on either side as it followed a small winding path that led down the hill. Gradually it went faster, and then faster still, until Gubble was far ahead, looking back at them and waving wildly.

"Keep going, Gubble!" Gracie called. "Tell them to put the kettle on!" She looked at Marcus and laughed. "I never thought we'd make it, did you?"

Marcus was looking over Gracie's shoulder, his eyes wide. "Gubble wasn't waving at us," he said hoarsely. "Look!"

Gracie turned, and there was Foyce.

Gracie screamed, and Foyce leaped, knocking Marcus off his feet and sending him rolling down the slope.

"Now you're mine, you little slug!" Foyce hissed, and lunged at Gracie.

Flinging herself to one side, Gracie scrabbled to get away, but she was too late. A hand had seized her ankle and was pulling her back. . . .

"AYEEEEEEEE!" Foyce's scream made the Ancient One sit bolt upright in her chair. The four princes and two princesses who were sipping tea in WATER WINGS froze. Elsie dropped her shuttle, and Val, leaning over the web, saw the dark stain fade. A great hope leaped inside her.

Gracie felt the grip on her ankle loosen and, wriggling free, saw that her stepsister was sinking slowly but inexorably into a sludge of wet sand.

"Help me!" Foyce shrieked. "Heeeeelp . . . !" And then, in front of Gracie's horrified eyes, there was nothing left of her but bubbles.

"It's OK, kiddo." Marlon was flying above the sand, grinning at Gracie. "She won't be hurt. They need her down at the house, see? She'll turn up in room thirteen. Remember? 'DO NOT ENTER UNLESS ABLE TO SWIM.' She'll be sandy between the toes all right, but fine." He winked at Gracie. "Until she meets the Ancient One, of course. Don't think much of her chances. Be a crone for *hundreds* of years if you ask me. Hey, there's a friend of yours come to get you!"

Gracie, shaky all over, looked down to where Marlon was pointing . . . and saw the path wriggling cheerfully at her feet. "Hello," she said, and stepped gently on.

With a surge of pure joy, the path swooped down and then up and then down again, and with the sensation of being on a particularly energetic roller coaster, Gracie found herself deposited at the door of the House of the Ancient Crones.

Chapter Thirty-three

The celebrations were subdued. Arry greeted Marcus with real gratitude and delight, but once the hugs were over, he was so very much inclined to put his arm around Princess Nina-Rose in a proprietorial fashion that Marcus had to work hard not to feel rejected. Prince Albion refused to stop being indignant and demanding decapitation for all and sundry, until at last the Ancient One sent a message asking him to come to room seventeen on his own. He came back looking pink and was obsequiously grateful to both Marcus and Gracie. Prince Tertius and Princess Fedora endlessly gazed lovingly into each other's eyes and took no notice whatsoever of their surroundings.

"Do you think they even noticed that they were turned into frogs?" Marcus asked under his breath. Gracie giggled and went on passing out chocolate cake.

Little Prince Vincent was the only one who was excited by his adventure. "Imagine me being a frog!" he kept saying. "Ribbit, ribbit!" Then he'd fall over laughing at his own joke until it was time to try it again. Gracie caught Marcus's eye, and he had to smother his laughter with a napkin.

When the irrepressible path had finally been persuaded to lie down and widen itself, and the royal carriages were able to come rolling up through the green mist, the Royal Families were reunited with hugs and tears.

"Well done, Marcus m'boy," King Frank boomed, over and over again. "Arioso says it's all thanks to you that he's back to normal! Well done, m'boy!"

"Actually," Marcus said, "it was much more Gracie. And—" He looked around for Gubble, but Gubble was nowhere to be seen.

"He's in hiding, kiddo," whispered Marlon, who was happily perched on Val's shoulder, with Millie on the other side.

"I'm sure the little lady was a great help," King Frank said, looking disapprovingly at the bats. "But we must be off! Hop into the carriage—there's a lad."

Marcus stood up straight and bowed. "Excuse me, Father, but I won't be coming back with you. Glee's here, so I shall ride him back later. Perhaps tomorrow or the day after. Please give my very best wishes to my mother, and"—he suddenly grinned hugely—"to Professor Scallio. Tell him the map was amazing."

King Frank looked long and hard at his second son. "Hmm," he said at last. "D'you know what? You've grown up, m'lad. Come back when you're ready." He tucked Nina-Rose's arm in his. "Oh—and about that map. Better keep it. Think you deserve it."

There was a wonderfully peaceful feeling in WATER WINGS after the princes and princesses had gone. Elsie sat back and helped herself to another piece of cake. "Wouldn't be royal if you paid me," she observed. "Don't know how you turned out so well, young Marcus."

Marcus shrugged. "I had a good tutor," he said, and glanced at Val. She looked anxious, but Marcus smiled. "He is your brother, isn't he?"

"Sure is," Val replied.

Marlon chipped in. "Best prof ever! Taught me everything I know!"

"And now we're going to live happily ever after, ain't we, Dad!" Millie said, and she fluttered a wing against Val's cheek.

Gracie began clearing up the plates and cups. "That's so nice," she said, and was pleased to note that she didn't sound at all wistful. "Happy-ever-afters are the best. . . . Oh! Where's Gubble?"

Elsie laughed. "He's in with the Ancient. They're talking about old times. She's promised him a cupboard in room four for his very own, and he's one happy troll."

Millie made a sudden swift zigzagging flight from Val to Gracie. "You'd be ever so welcome to come and share with us, Miss. Wouldn't she, Miss Val? And Dad?"

"Sure thing, kiddo," Marlon said. "Be a real pleasure. An honor. Absolutely."

"That's very kind of you," Gracie said slowly. "It really is. But I think, if it's OK, I might stay here for a while. If you'll have me, of course." She looked across at Elsie, who nodded reassuringly. "It's odd," Gracie went on, "but I kind of need to know that Foyce is all right . . . that she settles down as a crone. Is that silly?"

"Foyce?" Elsie stared at Gracie, then slapped her forehead. "Oh, my goodness me. If we haven't forgotten all about her. Just look at the time! She'll be about to pop up any moment! Marlon, be a good bat and warn the Ancient One. And Val—run back to the web so the Ancient's free!" She jumped up and hurried out of the room. After a moment's hesitation, Gracie followed her.

Outside room thirteen, Elsie paused with her hand on the door handle. "Are you sure you want to see her again, sweetie?" she asked. "She may be a little— shall we say—cross? Not dangerous, though. She'll be too sand-soaked for that."

"I'll be fine," Gracie said. All the same, she held her breath as Elsie opened the door and led the way into the room.

Chapter Thirty-four

At first Gracie thought it was an ordinary sitting room. There were a couple of cozy armchairs and a comfortable sofa, and a small but cheerful fire was burning in the grate. Only gradually did she notice that there were no windows and that what she had at first taken to be a brown circular rug in the middle of the floor wasn't a rug at all. It was a pool of wet sand, and from time to time a large bubble rose up, hovered on the surface, then popped.

"My word," Elsie said, "she *must* have been a bad 'un if she's taken this long to come through. Still, just as well. Wouldn't have been very nice for her to get here and find no welcome. Do have a seat, sweetie. May as well make ourselves comfy while we're waiting."

"Yes," Gracie agreed as she settled herself in an armchair. "Erm—where does she come from?"

"From there, of course." Elsie waved a hand at the sand pool. "Ooooh—looks like she might be on her way after all!"

The sand was beginning to bubble faster, and as Gracie watched in fascination, each bubble grew bigger than the one before.

"Won't be too long now," Elsie said. "Be a dear and give the Ancient a shout, will you?"

But Gracie didn't need to. The door opened, and the Ancient One wheeled herself in. "The web's all over the place," she announced, "so I knew it must be time. Ah . . . I was right!"

As Elsie and the Ancient One bent over the sand pool, Gracie took a step back. Something was beginning to emerge, something that looked as if it could be Foyce's head. Despite the wet sand, the golden curls were untouched, and as she continued to rise up, Gracie saw that Foyce was as clean and fresh as if she had just had a bath. She was dressed in snow-white clothes that seemed familiar; it took a moment for Gracie to realize they were Foyce's usual clothes but with all color drained out of them.

"Welcome to the House of the Ancient Crones, Miss Undershaft," Elsie said, and held out her hand.

Foyce ignored her. Her big blue eyes were fixed on

Gracie, but there was an element of uncertainty as well as cold fury in her expression. "I might have guessed this was all *your* fault, you little rat," she hissed. "And you'd better get me out of here, or—"

"Or what?" Elsie asked sweetly.

"Or she'll wish she'd never been born!" Foyce snapped.

"I fear," the Ancient One said slowly, "you will not be leaving us. Not for a long while. We have cleansed your clothes, but there are harder and much darker things that we must deal with, and these will take time. A long time."

Foyce stared disbelievingly at the Ancient One. "You can't keep me here," she snarled.

"Oh, but we can," said the Ancient One. "We can keep you here for as long as you need." And she turned the full force of her one blue eye on Foyce Undershaft.

Gracie had once left a tall candle too near the hearth, and the heat of the fire had caused the wax to gradually soften until it was drooping over. She was reminded of the candle as she watched Foyce wilt under the Ancient One's eye and meekly agree to follow Elsie into room seventeen.

The Ancient One watched her go with interest.

"She'll be a tough nut to crack," she said thoughtfully. "She'll fight back as soon as she's recovered, but we'll get there in the end."

"I do hope so," Gracie said.

The Ancient One chuckled. "You should have seen Elsie when she first came here. Robbed her grandparents, abandoned her mother, cheated her father, burned down orphanages by the dozen—and all with language you'd never believe! Now, leave that young woman to us, and you hop back to young Marcus."

Gracie nodded, and the Ancient One wheeled herself away to where Elsie was introducing Foyce to the intricacies of the weaving looms.

"You'll soon get the hang of it," Elsie told her. "We've got a nice little project for you to begin with. Black velvet, with blood-red petticoats. By the way, are you any good at embroidery?"

Foyce's only reply was a snort.

"I'll take that as a no," Elsie said. "Not to worry. Now, just sit yourself here. I'll tell you when you can get up again."

Chapter Thirty-five

Gracie found Marcus wiping down the table with surprising efficiency, Marlon and Millie making helpful suggestions as he did so.

"Hi," Gracie said, and lifted a pile of plates off a chair. "Foyce is here, but she's quite safe. She's been taken to the web room. She looks sort of . . . I don't know how to describe it. Kind of empty."

"That'll be the beginning," Marlon said chirpily. "Bad seeping out. Takes a while before the other grows in."

"It'll be odd living in the same house as Foyce and not having her shouting at me all the time," Gracie went on. "But I would like to stay here—for a while, anyway. It's strange. I lived in Fracture all my life, but that never felt like a real home. But this does."

Marcus took the plates from Gracie's hands. "Might you care to explore a bit from time to time?" he asked diffidently. "There are a lot of places on the map I'd like to see . . ."

"Sounds good to me," Gracie said, and her smile lit the room. She picked up the teapot. "But in the meantime, there's an awful lot of washing-up waiting to be done."

"OK," Marcus said. "You wash; I'll dry."

In room seventeen, the Ancient One watched as the last vestiges of gray faded from the web, leaving a smooth sheet of shining silver. "So *that's* all right," she said.

"It's nice to have a happy ending, isn't it?" Elsie agreed.

Foyce muttered something, but the Ancient One ignored her. "It is, Elsie," she said. "Very nice indeed. Let's hope it lasts. . . ."

In room four, Gubble grunted happily in his cupboard. "Gubble's Trouble gone," he said to himself, and then paused. An idea was seeping into his brain. An amazing idea. An idea that was so incredibly

brilliant that he had to close the cupboard door quickly in case it escaped and was lost forever.

"Gubble, Gubble—*got no Trouble!*" he said, and closed his eyes in ecstasy.

Out in the corridor, the purple quill was working overtime. THE END, it wrote. THE END THE END THEENDTHEENDTHEEND . . .

And it was.

Or was it?

Late one evening, a small bat came flipping over the balustrade of Lady Lamorna's castle as the old sorceress sat peacefully dreaming up unusual and unpleasant tasks for her new servant.

"I'm Alf," he said proudly. "Bat in training. Uncle Marlon's teaching me the tools of the trade, see, and I've brought a message!"

"Message?" Lady Lamorna asked. "What message?"

Alf puffed out his chest. "DRESS READY ALL COMPLETE STOP. SEND CASH PLUS DEPOSIT FOR DONKEY STOP. DELIVERY BY DONKEY AS SOON AS CASH RECEIVED STOP. PRICE DEDUCTION FOR LATE DELIVERY STOP. END OF MESSAGE STOP."

Alf, panting hard, perched himself on a twirl of ivy to recover.

Lady Lamorna smiled and went to find Mange's wooden brass-bound box. She counted out the gold into a small velvet bag and hung the bag around Alf's neck.

Alf fell backward into the darkness.

"Watch it, kiddo," said a voice from below. "Told ya to wait for me, didn't I? Heavy stuff, cash. Never mind. Millie—you ready? We'll do it easily with the three of us, but next time you're on your own, lad."

Lady Lamorna strode the battlements of her crumbling castle with a new spring in her step. The blood-red petticoats rustled in the most satisfactory manner, and the black velvet gown was patterned all over in silver with truly delightful spiders' webs and twists of poison ivy. The hem was deeply encrusted with more silver; embroidered skulls of every size and shape jostled each other for space, while silver-painted walnuts, looking for all the world like tiny skulls, clittered and clattered on the cold stone floors.

It would have taken a much sharper eye than Lady Lamorna's to see that the embroidery covered up many mistakes in the weaving—mistakes as if the weaver had been throwing the shuttle in a particularly angry fashion. . . .

Vivian French's writing career began in 1990 after many years of acting and storytelling. She writes across genres and age groups and has published dozens of highly acclaimed books for children, including *A Present for Mom; Growing Frogs; I Love You, Grandpa; T. Rex;* and *The Story of Christmas.* About *The Robe of Skulls,* the first book in the Tales from the Five Kingdoms series, she says, "I really hope children enjoy reading this story as much as I enjoyed writing it—I had FUN!" Vivian French lives in Scotland.